I0576346

# FEMDOM

*Dominant Sex With a Dom Female. How to Make Him Your Sex Slave. Turn Your Man Into a Quivering Sub. BDSM, Spanking Tactics...*

2

this book has been derived from various sources. Please consult a licensed professional before attempting any techniques outlined in this book.

By reading this document, the reader agrees that under no circumstances is the author responsible for any losses, direct or indirect, which are incurred as a result of the use of information contained within this document, including, but not limited to, — errors, omissions, or inaccuracies.

# Table of Contents

# Introduction

Welcome to the FEMDOM world! If this is your first time experiencing this type of relationship, then you are in for a treat. You will find that embracing your dominant nature is one of the most liberating experiences you can have in life. It's a means of acknowledging who you are, and most importantly, giving yourself the chance to express who you really want to be.

In this book, we are going to explore the FEMDOM dynamic, what this type of relationship is like, and how you can take your male partner from where they currently stand and turn them into your personal plaything. If that sounds too good to be true, then rest assured that it is far more common than you think.

If you have experienced the FEMDOM dynamic but want to explore it further, you will find a trove of information in this book that you won't easily find anywhere else. This book is meant to help you put the pieces together of a FEMDOM puzzle that will lead you to your ultimate desires.

We are going to explore what FEMDOM is, what it is all about, and how you can transform your man into an obedient sub. The fact of the matter is that there are no limits here. We will be testing your limits and those of your sub.

This volume is intended for women who are looking to embrace their dominant side. The techniques outlined in this book are meant to take your dominant self and put it to the test. While we won't be talking about purposely hurting your partner, we will be talking about inflicting as much pain as they can tolerate.

Don't worry; we won't be dealing with brutal, medieval torture. But we will be talking about the ways in which your man will gladly take pain and humiliation all because they enjoy it. If anything, they enjoy making you happy, and whatever makes you happy makes them happy.

This is quite a power rush.

So, if you're ready to explore your dominant side, then keep on reading. This book contains a progressive list of techniques that are meant to test your male submissive's limits. With each technique, you will grind their willpower into dust. Eventually, you will have a fully compliant submissive that will stop at nothing to please you.

If you believe that's too good to be true, you'd be surprised to find that it's actually quite common. There are plenty of men out there who wish for nothing more than to have a truly dominant woman do with them as she pleases. But in order to deliver on your expectations, you need to understand the ways of the FEMDOM dynamic. That's why this book is your ultimate guide to FEMDOM.

Please bear in mind that anything goes in the FEMDOM world so long as both partners mutually consent. This isn't about forcing your partner to do something they don't want to do. This is about getting

them to willingly accept your dominance over them...
and love it!

# Part I: Getting Started With FEMDOM

# Chapter 1: What Is FEMDOM and What it Is Not

There is a great deal of ideas surrounding FEMDOM in popular culture. In film, you generally see a leather-clad female pummeling a puny and insignificant male. In pornographic films, there is a varying degree of violence inflicted upon male submissives. Moreover, you find that these "subs" actually enjoy the pain they are receiving. In fact, it seems as though male subs seem to welcome the pain they feel.

The fact is that FEMDOM is a type of power dynamic that isn't necessarily like the depictions you see in film and pornography. FEMDOM is based on a power dynamic that is typical of all human relations. When you think about it, human society is based on hundreds of these power dynamics. These dynamics receive the name of "dominance hierarchies."

A dominance hierarchy implies that there is someone who controls others. Traditional hierarchies, particularly those seen in male-dominated societies, put women in a position of inferiority. This leads to women being subjugated to the will and desire of the males who control society. While discussing the abuse that women are subjected to in male-dominated societies is beyond the scope of this book, it's worth pointing out that modern society is geared toward giving women their rightful power back.

As such, FEMDOM is a dominance hierarchy in which a dominant woman exerts her influence over a submissive man. It is also important to point out that in this book, we are going to focus on a dominant female controlling a submissive male. This is an important distinction as there are FEMDOM relationships in which it is a dominant female and a submissive female. However, we won't be doing down that path in this volume.

## Dominant-Submissive Relationships

Generally speaking, all male-female relationships have some kind of power dynamic. As such, one of the partners is naturally more dominant than the other. When a dominant person enters a relationship with a naturally submissive person, the power dynamic tends to balance out. So, the naturally dominant individual has no trouble getting along with the submissive partner. In fact, the submissive partner welcomes the control that the dominant individual holds.

Regardless of whether the dominant individual is male or female, a relationship among a natural dominant and natural submissive makes things work out well enough. Things get complicated when two dominant individuals enter a relationship. This dynamic creates a power struggle in which both individuals want to subdue the other. This is quite common with a dominant female and a "regular" male. Even if a regular male isn't a naturally dominant, there is always a degree of resistance on their part to the dominance exerted by the female. This is both instinctive and culture. After all, it's not "cool" to accept, as a man, that they are dominated by a female.

This power struggle generally leads to the deterioration of the relationship unless the female gives up trying to be dominant, or the male accepts that they are not naturally dominant and should assume a more submissive role. Such outcomes are hard to come by, particularly as a dominant female should not have to compromise for the sake of making an insecure male "happy."

## What Is a FEMDOM Relationship?

So, defining FEMDOM takes us down a path of the sexual dynamic that occurs between males and females. Typically, males are expected to be dominant in the bedroom. Now, this by no means implies that violence by a male on a female is justified. What this does imply is that the male is expected to lead the interaction among the couple during sexual intercourse. When the male is unable to lead, then the female is left with the task of leading the way. If the female is not naturally dominant, then this might create serious issues for the couple in question.

Generally speaking, the power dynamic from the relationship itself tends to carry over into the bedroom. This means that if the male is naturally dominant and the female is naturally submissive, then this dynamic will carry over into the bedroom. On the contrary, if the female is naturally dominant and the male is naturally submissive, then this dynamic should also carry over into the bedroom.

The challenge then becomes to get the submissive male to embrace the fact that they should follow the lead of a female in all matters sexual. This female dominance can be reflected in something as simple as having the female initiate intercourse. Furthermore, it can be expanded into something as broad as female dominants exerting violence and pain into their submissive male.

The FEMDOM relationship is born when the man accepts that they are submissive and that their female dominant (also referred to as a "dom" or "dominatrix") is the one in charge of the entire sexual dynamic. This dynamic can then extend to whatever levels the couple feels comfortable with. In some cases, submissive males simply seek a female dom as a "power figure." Other male submissives (henceforth referred to as "subs") seek a maternal figure. In other words, they want to be "babied" by their dom. This is seen in some films in which the male dresses up as a baby and crawls around on the floor.

Also, FEMDOM relationships can extend into the world of BDSM. This is a domain which we will explore in this book with great detail. It should be noted that the typical definition of a dominatrix is a female who literally reduces a man into dust. This is where BDSM can be used to practically humiliate a man into the lowest common denominator. Of course, we're not espousing violence or belittling anyone. Yet, the power dynamic that emerges between a

12

dominatrix and her subs takes on some very wild overtones. And yes, professional dominatrices tend to have multiple subs.

## The psychology of FEMDOM Relationships

A FEMDOM relationship is predicated on the psychological factors that lead a male sub to accept their submissiveness. By the same token, a female dom must embrace her dominance. This implies breaking the traditional societal role that places women as the "weak" sex. Women can be just as dominant or even more so than men. As such, female doms must embrace their dominance so that they can fully derive the pleasure that comes with exerting their dominance over males.

As for males, the first step is to acknowledge their submissiveness. This step is by far the most significant step that a man can take in their journey toward becoming the sub that they truly are. Then, a female dom can go about teaching a male sub in the ways of becoming a true sub.

At this point, we will look at two different perspectives.

First, let's consider a committed relationship (boyfriend-girlfriend or husband-wife). In this type of relationship, the male accepts that their female partner is the dom. As such, the male then relinquishes their control over to the female with the understanding that she has his best interest in mind and that everything that happens between them is of mutual consent. This is very important as the intention here is to break down the male's resistance. If the male is not completely on board, then the chances of the relationship working out are slim. Of course, there is always some kind of resistance at the beginning, but then again, that's what the exercises in this book are all about.

Second, let's consider a non-committed relationship. Under this concept, we can take those relationships in which the interaction is solely based on sex or those relationships which are casual, a type of "friends with benefits" arrangement, so to speak. In this type of relationship, the interaction is based solely on sex, and thus the female dom must be ready to exert all of her influence on the male sub. In these types of relationships, males tend to purposely seek out female doms so that they can directly engage in this type of relationship. In some cases, inexperienced male subs may seek out an experienced female dom to "teach" them the ways of being a sub. Under these circumstances, the male sub will be far more willing to accept being submissive.

Whether you are in a committed or non-committed relationship, it's best to lay down the ground rules first. There needs to be a clear consensus about what the relationship entails, and most importantly, how far the male is willing to go. Limits and boundaries are important. However, it is just as important for males to accept that they must be willing to push their own boundaries.

A good way of looking at boundaries in a FEMDOM relationship is by comparing them to a regular BDSM relationship. Both the dom and the sub have their boundaries. These boundaries must be respected at all times. Anything beyond that can be agreed to mutually. This is important to ensure both safety and pleasure.

## What a FEMDOM Is Not

A dom-sub relationship is not synonymous with an abusive relationship. A first glance, the boundaries between a dom-sub relationship and an abusive one tends to be quite blurry. But when you drill down, you will find that there is a clear distinction.

An abusive relationship is generally defined as one partner, causing harm to the other. This means that the abuser says and does things to the victim, which causes them physical and psychological harm. This includes assault, sexual abuse, and psychological distress. Such relationships are unacceptable and should be ended immediately. Sadly, traditional cultural perception places a sub-dom relationship, such as BDSM, as "mutually-agreed violence."

Consequently, FEMDOM is not some type of weak justification for a female to purposely harm males. Yes, there is a high degree of aggression involved, particularly in torture techniques. And yes, there is a high degree of masochism on the part of the sub, but at the end of the day, both parties are perfectly aware of the events taking place and are in perfect agreement. This is why consent is fundamental. In some cases, paperwork is signed in order to ensure mutual consent.

FEMDOM relationships are also a means of allowing both males and females to explore this sexuality. As such, a FEMDOM relationship is not a female using "mind control" over a male. This may be hard for casual observers to understand. Deep down, subs want to be dominated. They want to be humiliated. They want to be tortured. In a manner of speaking, it's like deriving pleasure from pain. By the same token, the dom has a sadistic side to them as they derive pleasure from inflicting pain on their sub.

Sure, we could go into the psychological and emotional causes of this behavior. But the fact of the matter is we are simply acknowledging reality. A female dom derives pleasure from exerting their influence over a male, while a male sub derives pleasure from being subjugated to the will and desire of a female.

One rather interesting explanation for this behavior lies in the fact that people who are in positions of power tend to become overwhelmed with responsibility. As such, having intimate encounters in which they are free to surrender power over to someone else can prove to be liberating. However, there is a caveat here: anyone who is truly dominant will do anything in their power to avoid relinquishing power. As such, they will try their hardest to keep control. Often, this implies going to great lengths in order to remain in control of the situation, and the people, around them.

Ultimately, a FEMDOM relationship is about what both partners want to get out of it. For one, it's the rush of power, while for the other, it's the pleasure of being dominated. And while this is clearly a balance of power dynamic, at the end of the day, if it makes all participants happy, then so be it. Who are we to judge what makes others feel good about themselves? The goal here is to provide useful information that can lead to a happier and more enjoyable sex life.

# Chapter 2: Why Turn Your Man Into Your Plaything?

As a woman, exploring your dominant side may not be the easiest thing to do. After all, social conditioning has forced women into the submissive and agreeable role even when they are not naturally inclined to be that way.

As a matter of fact, being a dominant woman can be hard, especially when considering how insecure men turn out to be. This makes it tough for men to accept their submissive nature (unless they are naturally dominant). Now, it should be noted that by "dominant," we mean that a man is not only comfortable in their own skin, but they are also naturally inclined to lead. This has nothing to do with being the loudest guy in the gym or the meanest dude on the block.

That being said, your desire to embrace your dominant nature means that submissive men will naturally gravitate toward you. Even "dominant" guys will gravitate toward you when they see that you are naturally dominant. But what should you do with a guy like this?

It really depends on what you want to get out of a relationship. For some ladies, being in charge is enough of a power rush. They feel satisfied in knowing that they are in control of their partner. For others, they feel satisfied bossing their man around. This feeling is especially heightened when they are able to get him to do what she wants when she wants it.

But then, there are women who want more. They may be in full control of their relationship, but there is always something more that they would like to get out of it. That's why we are going to discuss five reasons why you should go all the way into turning your man into your personal plaything. After all, if you are both down with the dom-sub power dynamic, then why not go all the way?

## Reason #1: You Both Enjoy It

As with any type of sexual relationship, there needs to be consent from both parties. If this is the case, then there should be no reason for either of you to hold back. If anything, you both ought to embrace a FEMDOM dynamic.
Why not?

If he is at least willing to give it a try, then there is no reason why you shouldn't pursue it further. The fact is that a man who acknowledges that the woman in his life is the "boss" isn't far away from being a good sub. Given the fact that a FEMDOM relationship is essentially an emotional and psychological bond, you both have everything to gain from this type of relationship.

In addition, dom-sub relationships generally involved a sadistic/masochistic component. As such, both partners get intense pleasure from the relationship itself. The difference lies in the perspective of the relationship. As a result, the sub derives their pleasure from seeing their sub go through any number of situations while the sub feels pleasure from being subjected to the treatment their dom inflicts upon them.

Now, there is an important element here: the sub is not attracted to the treatment per se; they are attracted to being treated in this manner by the dom. It's kind of like enjoying a cheeseburger, but it isn't just any cheeseburger; it's the cheeseburger from a specific restaurant.

This is exactly what happens in a FEMDOM relationship. You man isn't attracted to pain, humiliation, and torture itself. He is attracted to YOU, inflicting this type of treatment on him. This is what makes it so pleasurable. While he might be willing to engage in this type of relationship with someone else, to him, it's doing it with you that unleashes the full submissive experience.

So, as long as you are both enjoying the dynamic, then have at it! There is no reason for you to hold back. If anything, resolve to try new things. Make a concerted effort to push your boundaries as much as possible. You never know what heights of pleasure you can hit.

## Reason #2: He Asked for It

Every time a man enters a FEMDOM relationship, it's because he asked for it. A man is never forced into a FEMDOM relationship. Even if he is a victim of sexual assault of some nature (which usually happens at the hand of another man), he will seek to be in a FEMDOM relationship. This is something that he wants, even if he can't consciously articulate.

This implies that your man, while perfectly willing to be in a FEMDOM relationship with you, won't come out directly and say, "Hey babe, I think it's time we had a FEMDOM thing around here." So, he may not necessarily say it with words, but he will totally say it with his attitude and his behavior.

How can you spot this disposition?

There are a number of subtle and not so subtle clues that will tell you what's going on in his mind.

First, you can easily tell a man is submissive by the way he lets you lead things in the bedroom. Often, submissive men allow women to dictate what happens during intercourse. This can be something as simple as letting her decide when penetration occurs when oral play happens, or even when he orgasms. In other cases, submissive men are perfectly comfortable with letting the woman make demands from him no matter how outrageous they may seem. These are the guys that are willing to dress up a clown if that turns his partner on.

Next, submissive men show some kind of fear toward women. Now, this isn't the type of fear in which they hide under the bed (at least not early on...), but it does become manifest when things get hot and heavy. For instance, these types of men are unable to react appropriately when a woman shows signs of arousal. They are simply unable to take charge and lead the way. In fact, they may sit there waiting for orders.

Lastly, dominant women are a turn on for these kinds of men. The turn-on occurs when the woman exerts her influence on the man through any number of ways. For example, these men are happy to be penetrated by their female partner. These men find pleasure and satisfaction in being penetrated by their female partner through the use of a strap-on or dildo. You might think that these men are really homosexual. However, we're talking about perfectly heterosexual men who enjoy the submission that occurs when they are penetrated by a woman.

So, don't be surprised to find your man asking to be dominated. The signs are there. All you have to do is be on the lookout for them.

## Reason #3: Power Is Addictive

There is a reason why dictators go to great lengths to hold onto power. It's because they become addicted to it. Simply put, power is intoxicating. It produces an overwhelming feeling of superiority over someone or something. This feeling might be a bit too much at first, but over time, the rush that comes with having control makes it impossible to let go.

The same goes for the FEMDOM world. When you experience the rush that comes from completely and utterly dominating someone, you become addicted to it. While it's not like getting high on drugs, it certainly produces a need for more and more of it. This is where doms are tempted to push their subs farther and farther. In general, subs go along with it because they won't really question what their doms want, that is, unless they feel threatened.

Also, FEMDOM relationships offer something that "traditional" relationships don't offer: a balance of power. There are women who are constantly competing in a "man's world." Often, this constant competition leads to a feeling of exhaustion. After all, it's not easy having to justify being in a position of power in the business world all the time. So, the FEMDOM dynamic affords you the opportunity to be in charge without being questioned by others. There is no second-guessing in FEMDOM. Your sub is perfectly willing to go along because they trust you and follow you. As such, you can really be yourself without the need to justify it all the time.

## Reason #4: You Are Comfortable With Running the Show All the Time

Being a dom means you have to be in charge all the time. That's just the nature of the game. If you have a sub at your feet, your sub won't move a finger unless you tell them to. This can be tiresome, especially if you are meticulous and want to plan everything down to the slightest details.

There are some women who are just like that. They need to have everything planned out to the slightest detail. They cannot afford to let anything escape their attention. As a result, being in charge of everything, all the time, can be draining.

You see, there is no such thing as delegating responsibility in the FEMDOM world. You are in charge of everything, and your man has no choice but to go along for the ride. Otherwise, they can hit the road. It's as simple as that. So, you must be comfortable with the idea of being in charge of everything, even if it means be overburdened at times by it.

Consider this situation:

Your partner is fully committed to letting you run everything the way you see fit. As such, you need to tell your partner what they are going to wear, how they are going to please you, and what they need to do in order to be pleased. For example, you must tell your partner when to perform oral sex on you and when they can penetrate you. While this may sound scripted (to a certain degree it is), the truth is that you can't really improvise. Otherwise, you run the risk of missing out on a truly pleasurable experience.

In addition, holding power also means protecting your partner as well. Since they are in a vulnerable position all the time, you need to make sure that whatever happens needs to as safe as possible. For instance, if your partner likes choking, then you better be sure you don't take it too far.

# Reason #5: It's just fun

Then, there is the simplest reason of them all: it's just fun being in charge. After all, who doesn't like being the boss?

It's fun to be the one who dictates what is to be done and when it should be done. If you can't find pleasure in holding someone's entire life in your hands, then FEMDOM might not be the best for you. In fact, you have so much power over your sub that you could basically kill them without any resistance.

This is where the essence of the power rush comes from.

Yet, it's so much fun to know that during that encounter, you are the master of your corner of the universe. The best part of all is that your partner is perfectly willing to remain powerless. They are perfectly comfortable with the idea of relinquishing any kind of resistance. They know that by submitting to you, they will obtain the ultimate pleasure they seek.

Now that is powerful stuff.

At the end of the day, the FEMDOM dynamic is fun for both the dom and the sub. As long as both parties are perfectly clear on the nature of the dynamic, there should be no reason why the both of you can't have the time of your lives. Each encounter is meant to give you the opportunity to explore your innermost nature. It is during these encounters that you have a safe space in which you can be yourselves. There is no one judging what you are doing. This is incredibly liberating.

So, if you are truly into FEMDOM, then go for it! The last thing you want to do is to spend your life trying to play a role you weren't to play.

# Chapter 3: Are You Ready for FEMDOM?

Being the dom in a FEMDOM relationship sounds pretty simple. If anything, it sounds exciting to be the one in control all the time. At this point, it might sound exciting to have a puny little man groveling at your feet while they are compelled to cater to your whims.

However, that's only a part of the game. Being a dom is so much more than that. It's not merely a question of having sex slaves doing your bidding. It's about using your dominance in such a way that the relationship is self-sustaining and provides both of you with the pleasure you seek. That's why being a dom is much more than just wearing leather and walking around with a flogger.

By definition, a dom is someone who is powerful, imposing, and relishes in taking control of a situation. A true dom doesn't need to be led by anyone. A dom instinctively takes charge of a situation even if they don't know what to do. You see this type of behavior all the time in all facets of life. In business, doms let their character shine as they naturally draw others around them. These are true leaders who others tend to look to.

This type of personality easily translates into the bedroom. In the bedroom, true doms are able to take their partner on a journey of pleasure. Regardless of the nature of the relationship, the sub is perfectly willing to be led as they trust their dom's judgment.

However, doms tend to be confused with bullies. Often, you see films in which there are "doms" beating up defenseless subs such as in BDSM. This gets worse when the sub is forced into doing things they are not comfortable with. This is abuse and must not be tolerated. You can't expect to be a dom by forcing someone to do something they don't want to do. You can't be considered a dom simply because you are in a position of power.

A true dom is always concerned about their sub's wellbeing. In some BDSM relationships, the dom is in charge of every aspect of the sub's life. This includes making sure they eat properly, get enough rest, and exercise regularly. It may sound like a parent running a child's life, but the fact of the matter is that a true dom is committed to making sure that their sub is safe and feels secure.

We won't be going that far in this book. The scope of this book is not focused on the dom-sub relationship outside of the bedroom. But we do want to emphasize that being a true dom means that you are willing to act in a way that will always ensure your sub's wellbeing while respecting whatever boundaries you have set.

With that in mind, here are five ways to recognize if you are a true dom.

## Sign #1: Most People Let You Take Control of Things

A true dom is a leader in all aspects of life. The true dom is perfectly comfortable with taking responsibility. So, people recognize this and automatically let the dom take over. You see, being dominant is about taking responsibility for the circumstances surrounding a situation. In the workplace, true doms take on the responsibility of getting a job done on time, even when they are not the supervisor. If anything, the supervisor might be a "fake dom," that is, they hide behind their job title to boss people around. But they are not a true dom as they would rather delegate responsibility on others.

In the bedroom, a true dom takes responsibility for their pleasure and that of their partners. This is important to bear in mind as a common misconception of a dom is that they seek selfish pleasure.

That could not be farther from the truth.

Another common misconception is that the sub is actually suffering while in the submissive role. Observers believe that a sub who is being humiliated is being forced into something they don't like.

That's completely false!

A true sub enjoys being subjected to a lower rank. They derive pleasure from being put into a position of inferiority. Otherwise, they wouldn't willingly accept this kind of relationship. Moreover, they would run away as fast as they can the first chance they got.

So, embracing your true dominant personality means that you are perfectly willing to lead your partner(s) to their own pleasure while you help them pleasure you. It's a win-win as everyone derives the pleasure they seek from the FEMDOM dynamic.

## Sign #2: You Have Power Even When You Are Not in a Position of Authority

Contrary to what most people think, power isn't something that you can just grab. You might be able to take on a position of authority by force, but people will never recognize your power. Power is something that people willingly relinquish to someone else. This is why charismatic leaders have a huge following. It seems as though people gladly acknowledge they hold the power.

In a FEMDOM relationship, you don't need to beat your partner senseless in order to get them to acknowledge your dominance. Male subs automatically acknowledge their FEMDOM's power over them. It's a natural occurrence. You don't need to threaten male subs. They will willingly go along with you. There is no need for any external coercion. It may seem paradoxical, but it's just a natural process.

Now, you might encounter men who are attracted to the idea of being a sub. But, they are either wrestling with internal issues with regard to this, or they are simply not ready to let go. This is where the training process you can provide for them is intended to progressively let them get over their hang-ups in such a way that they can progressively embrace their submissive nature, until one day, they are nothing more than your personal slaves.

However, this is a personal process. You can't really force anyone to be a sub. Yes, you can force them into a submissive role, but they won't enjoy it. If anything, you'll probably kill them first before they are truly able to respond to your dominance. Sure, there are folks (male and female) who get a twisted pleasure from harming others. However, the truth FEMDOM gets her pleasure as a result of the pleasure subs get from feeling pain, humiliation, torture, and so on. If you are familiar with BDSM relationships, then you can totally appreciate this dynamic.

## Sign #3: People Look to You When There Is Trouble

This sign isn't directly related to the bedroom, but it's a great way of telling just how dominant you really are. When people automatically look to you when something is wrong, it means that people recognize the fact that you have power. These folks understand that they can count on you as you are not afraid to take the lead. Also, it is because you have demonstrated that you have taken on responsibility at various points in your life.

When you meet new potential sexual partners, they will automatically sniff out your dominant nature. As such, the "dominant" males (not the true dominant males) will try to avoid you. Fake doms are generally insecure males. As such, they will try to avoid you as much as they can.

However, those males who are already cognizant of their submissive nature will gravitate toward you automatically. But this doesn't mean that they are weak. In fact, they could be highly competent men. What it means is that they simply seek a female dom who can provide them with the female force they seek.

Plain and simple.

If you are in a relationship at the moment, don't be surprised if you are the one who makes all the decisions. If you find that your partner is perfectly willing to follow your lead, then don't be surprised to find that they will not object to an increasing level of submission. That's where this guide can help you take your man further and further down the road to full submission.

## Sign #4: Your Sexual Partners Don't Resist Your Lead

When you find yourself having intercourse with a male partner, you might be surprised to find that they offer very little resistance to your lead. For instance, when you ask them to perform oral on you, they willingly oblige. Then, when you ask them to penetrate you, they gladly do it. After, you ask them to pull out and touch you, and they quickly follow suit. This type of attitude is a clear indication that you are dealing with a submissive man. The situation is heightened when the man simply stands by until you command them. In fact, some men will even go as far as resist orgasm until the woman tells them it's okay to do so.

If that seems strange to you, perhaps you haven't really taken the lead in your relationships.

When you consciously take the lead, the man in your relationship will either try to fight back or give in. Now, if you are dealing with a naturally dominant male, he will not give you much of a chance to lead. He will automatically take charge, and that's that. At that point, it's up to you to follow his lead or offer resistance of your own.

Naturally, dominant males like to lead all the time. They have no trouble in taking a woman by the hand and leading them on the journey to mutual pleasure. A naturally dominant male will do everything he can to give his partner the best experience possible.

This doesn't happen with "fake doms." Fake doms like to boss girls around in pursuit of their selfish pleasure.

The dame dynamic applies to true FEMDOMS. The true FEMDOM simply takes charge and doesn't ask questions. The male can then follow suit or find someone else. When you really think about it, it's really that cut and dry.

## Sign #5: You Don't Have a Big Ego

One of the key characteristics of a fake dom is that they talk a big game. These are the types (both male and female) who like to brag about their experience. They like to boast about how they don't put up with crap from anyone, blah, blah, blah.

A true dom doesn't have to say much to make their presence felt. They also don't have a big ego.

Think about that for a minute.

If you don't have a big ego, you don't have the need to talk a big game. You know who you are, what you are capable of, and you are confident you can deliver all the time. Your partner(s), in turn, will quickly acknowledge this. They will seek you out because they know that they are guaranteed to have a great time every time they are with you.

This isn't even about looks. Sure, it helps to be attractive, but then again, what good is a pretty face if they are shallow and selfish?

This is why the true dom makes their presence felt just by being who they are. There is no need for any fluff. It's all substance. This is why there is no need for a big ego. If anything. A big ego is just a means of overcompensating for shortfalls. While this is rather common among men, women are also guilty of this from time to time.

So, it's always a good idea to keep your ego in check. You don't need to pretend to be humble or even submissive. All you need to do is let your actions speak for themselves. The rest will fall into place. At the end of the day, you know who you are and what you are capable of. You are interested in attracting men who want the same things as you. So, don't waste your time with people who are pretending to be something they are not.

# Chapter 4: Is Your Man Ready for FEMDOM?

Is your man, or any man in your life, for that matter, ready for FEMDOM?

That is a very interesting question...

It might be hard to tell. In fact, you may never really know until you actually go down that road. You see, most men, while willing to go along with a FEMDOM relationship, may have never actually experienced one. So, they won't really know what to look for.

In some cases, you might find a man who already has experience in this type of relationship. In that case, it's easier to deal with them. It could be that they've tried it, but never really had someone to lead them and teach them the ways of FEMDOM.

You can't expect a man to know what to do unless someone teaches. FEMDOM is not the kind of thing that you can learn on your own, at least from the sub's point of view. This is the type of thing you need to learn on your own. As a matter of fact, even if a man is an experienced sub, doms have different attitudes and personalities. As such, this means that you need to mold your man, or men, into the way you want them to be. This is why there can never be two identical FEMDOM experiences for a male sub.

This means that it's your job to take your man and turn him into the male sub you want him to be.

However, you need to keep in mind that he needs to be ready to give in and embrace his role as a sub. You can't force him to accept this role. Otherwise, you would be breaking his will. This would lead to disastrous consequences as he wouldn't relish the role that you would put him in. The whole idea is to turn him into a willing sub. Thus, he needs to see how much pleasure he can derive from pleasing you in every possible manner.

So, in this chapter, we are going to take a look at five signs that will tell you if your man is really ready to become your sub.

## Sign #1: He Doesn't Question Anything You Say or Do

This sign applies to every aspect of your life. While it doesn't mean that your man has blind faith in you, it just means that he's willing to accept anything you say and do without putting up much of a fight.

With this sign, there is one important element.

When you are a highly competent woman, you're much more likely to make smart decisions and avoid making major mistakes. While nothing is perfect, you get it right most of the time. This builds credibility and reliability on your end. So, your man won't have much to complain about the way you go about life.

A great example of this is money management. If you find that you are much more efficient at managing money than your partner, and he does not question any of your decisions, especially because you have shown to be competent, then you can be sure that he will go along with your decisions in the bedroom.

While money is just one of the many examples in which you can see just how much influence you have over your partner, it goes to show that he is ready to be led... by you. It's important to note that he may never be able to have a FEMDOM relationship with anyone else by you. You see, he trusts you. He follows you. So, he may never have the same type of feelings toward anyone else. He'll be willing to open up to you. But you must show him the way. His naturally submissive nature will not allow him to discover FEMDOM on his own. If anything, he'll be afraid to go outside of your relationship out of fear of upsetting you.

In the event you meet someone new, you can easily tell if they are submissive. All you have to do is boss them around. It could be that they will go along with everything you say out of desperation. But then again, if you find that he is unable to look at you straight in the eye, he can't interject during a conversation, and can't seem to work up the nerve to ask you about anything, then it could be that you have a natural sub on your hands.

It would then be up to you to pursue a dom-sub relationship further.

# Sign #2: He Accepts Orders

This sign is pretty straightforward. You are the boss, and he obeys orders. Now, we're not talking about bossing your man around. We're talking about commanding him as if you were in the army. It's one thing to tell your man to do something he's been putting of for a while. And, it's another entirely different thing to command your desires.

For instance, during sex, you tell him exactly what you want him to do. You tell him where to touch you, how to touch, and when to touch you. And he is perfectly fine with this! You don't see him trying to go for his pleasure ahead of yours. If you ask him to sit by the bedside and wait until you are ready for him, he will gladly do it.

Some folks confuse this attitude with a lack of character. They make it out to be that he is "not a real man" or that he is "pussy whipped." Unfortunately for most men, the typical male stereotype of the "macho alpha" isn't really applicable. The vast majority of men will never truly exhibit the traits of the so-called "alpha male." In fact, the alpha male is a superior kind of male that isn't easily bred. This type of male is not the biggest, loudest, and strongest (at least not physically). This is the kind of man that isn't afraid to be vulnerable, yet strong enough to deal with life's adversities head on.

Do you see where we are going with this?

So, if your man isn't exactly alpha male material, it does mean he isn't a "real man." It's just that his personality is not suited to be the one leading the charge.

This is where you come in. You have total control over the dynamic in your relationship, and if he is perfectly fine with accepting a submissive role, then so be it. Take full advantage of your dominant nature and his submissive demeanor to build a dynamic in which he doesn't have to pretend to be strong, and you don't have to pretend to be weak.

## Sign #3: He Always Puts Your Needs Ahead of His

While it is true that dominant men are perfectly capable of putting others' needs ahead of their own, a submissive man will never go out of his way to satisfy himself without your approval.

Consider this situation:

A submissive man will not dare go out to boys' night because he is afraid that you won't approve of his friends. Now, the difference here is that a weak man is just afraid of standing up for himself. A sub will think about pleasing you first, and then if you approve, he will go out with his friends.

Do you see the difference?

When you translate this attitude into the bedroom, your sub will always be at your beck and call. If you ask him to give you oral first until the cows come home, he will gladly do it. Then, you can "reward" him by doing what you know he likes. In this case, you are not doing what he wants; you are being generous enough to grant him what he likes. He'll be perfectly happy to work hard for his reward because, in his mind, your happiness and satisfaction are first.

Perhaps the biggest difference between a dominant and submissive male is that a truly dominant male will put the wellbeing of others before his. However, the dominant male understands that it is important for him to take care of himself for the sake of those he protects. As such, a dominant male is protective. The submissive male seeks protection. It may not be physical, but certainly emotional. This is where the emotional connection of a FEMDOM relationship is so strong.

That is why you should not frown upon your male sub's need for protection. If anything, you lose nothing by giving it to him. All he wants is to know that you have everything under control in such a way that he can let go of himself and be free to enjoy his sexuality.

## Sign #4: He Seeks Your Approval During Sex

This sign ties perfectly well into the previous one. A naturally submissive male will always ask for your approval during sex. Whenever he does anything, he wants to know if this is something you like, something that you enjoy. So, he will constantly seek validation during intercourse.

In this case, you often get questions like, "am I going too fast?" or "do you like what I'm doing?"

Now, you might be thinking, "just shut up and do it!"

But don't get upset. In fact, cut the poor guy a break. He just wants to do things right by you. He wants to make sure that you are enjoying things as much as he is. The difference lies in the fact that he either doesn't know how to go about things or would much rather have you tell him what you want, when you want it and where you want it.

If you are comfortable with giving him a blueprint to your body, then the good news is that you will be guaranteed a good time, every time. Even when he can't "rise to the occasion," you can always find something for him to do. Oddly enough, that is liberating for men.

Think about that for a moment.

In those times in which a man cannot have an erection, it can be liberating to know that the female will not chastise him for his lack of virility. In fact, she will find alternatives for him to get the job done. In these cases, "punishment" is used. One such example could be a humiliating activity like licking the soles of your shoes.

So, cut your subs a break. They just want to please you.

## Sign #5: He Is Willing to Accept an Open Relationship

This has got to be the biggest sign of them all.

Why?

Well, because he is willing to go along with an open relationship on your end, but not his. He is not allowed to see anyone else unless you approve of it. However, you do not need to seek his approval to see someone else.

This is where dominatrices end up having relationships with multiple men. All men know that the dominatrix has other men (perhaps they just don't know who they are), and they are perfectly fine with it.

A great example of this is cuckoldry. In this technique, the female dom has sex in front of her sub. This technique is used as a means of humiliation. The male sub has no choice but to sit by and watch. Depending on how far the female dom wants to take it, the male sub might be required to perform sexual acts on the other male. This is particularly humiliating if the sub is not homosexual or does not enjoy sexual activity with other males.

Ultimately, if your sub will not question you for having an open relationship on your end, then you know you have a truly submissive male on your hands. So, do take the time to pose this situation on the table. If you find that he will not put up resistance, then just make sure that you acknowledge his feelings by giving him the reassurance that he needs. Mainly, if you are in a committed relationship, make him feel safe in that you won't leave him for someone else. All you are doing is just having some fun in your free time.

# Part II: Easing Into FEMDOM

# Chapter 5: Basic FEMDOM Tactics

One of the most important roles of any FEMDOM is to groom her male subs the way she wants them to be. Since male subs aren't born knowing how to be the right sub, they need to learn how to become one. And even if you found an experienced sub, he'll be molded to his previous dom's ways. Needless to say, your ways are naturally going to be different.

Also, if you happen to have a newbie on your hands, then it's up to you to train him in the way you expect him to act. You can't just expect him to figure out what to do. As such, it's part of your role to set the rules, establish guidelines, and enforce them.

At this point, it's important to note that there needs to be consequences every time your sub transgresses your wishes. To provide "punishment," you can implement any of the tactics we are going to describe in the remaining parts of this book.

However, one very powerful tactic is to withhold what gives him the most pleasure. For instance, if your sub enjoys penetrating you, then you can choose to withhold this from him until he is fully compliant. In a manner of speaking, it can serve as a treat for a job well done.

In that regard, you too, will learn to recognize your sub's demeanor. As you see what really gets his motor running, you will be able to use it as both an advantage and as a means of controlling him. Please remember that the name of the game is control. If you do not assert your dominance from the get-go, you will never be able to fully master your sub.

In this chapter, we are going to start things off slowly. We are going to describe tactics that are more psychological than sexual. These tactics are meant to assert your position and teach him the rules of the game. You can then choose if this will lead to sex, or just remain as part of the training. If anything, you could ask him to please you while he has to wait his turn.

## Teaching Your Sub Some Manners

What is a FEMDOM relationship without proper manners?

Your sub needs to understand that you are the master and should address you accordingly. The use of proper manners is a powerful psychological technique that is intended to instill in him the respect that he must observe for you. You cannot expect him to automatically address you and treat you the way you desire. This is something that he must learn. So, you are there to gladly teach him. In addition, never forget that he's there to please you at all times...

A good way to get things started is to let him know he must use "please" and "thank you" at all times. He will not be allowed to do anything unless he politely requests permission. **This is very important**. He cannot be allowed to do anything unless he requests and is granted permission.

For example, if he wishes to touch himself, or you, for that matter, he must ask for permission. If he touches himself in an attempt to pleasure himself, that would be considered a transgression, and a penalty would ensure.

If he is granted permission to touch himself, say to masturbate, he must thank you properly for allowing him to do so. Otherwise, he would be nothing more than an ungrateful worm of a man.

Additionally, make sure he addresses you the way you wish him to do so. Some common ways are "mistress," "ma'am," or "madam." If you choose to take up a dom name, say "Madam Pain," then make sure he addresses you properly. Otherwise, it's going to be time-out for him!

## Serving You

Another important part of being an obedient sub is to serve you just the way you like it. A good way to kick things off is to have him serve you food and drink. He can play the role of the slave serving their mistress.

Now, you can take this as far as you would like. You can give him explicit orders about what you want him to do for you. You can ask him to paint your nails or shave your body. You can even take it further and add humiliating requests such as cleaning up a bathroom mess. Remember that he must obey your orders to the letter. In exchange, he might get a small treat, say masturbation, or perhaps pleasuring you.

However, don't allow him to enjoy himself at first. As such, try to avoid intercourse during this time. Otherwise, it will build an expectation that he will get sex every time. That is clearly not the case; you will not allow him to do what he likes just because he did what you said.

That is expected of him. After all, it's the least he could do.

## Sissy Play

This is the first time we are going to explore sissy play. In essence, this technique involves getting him to do "girly" things. One easy yet effective way of getting a sub to learn his place is to have him wear make-up. Of course, you won't be doing any of it. He'll be doing it himself. So, he had better learn how to do his make-up properly.

Once he has done his make-up, you can be the judge. If he has done things to your satisfaction, you might consider giving him a treat. It's entirely up to you. Another interesting tactic is to have him watch a guy on guy porn with you. This is especially useful if he has not shown any interest in men. This will allow you to create an interesting visual for yourself while he gets to take a walk down his sissy side.

Please keep in mind that male subs fantasize about their feminine side. Some might act upon it, while others may not feel entirely comfortable. So, if you give him the chance to explore his girly side, it could end up being a huge turn-on for him. As such, don't be afraid to encourage his girly side. The likelihood that is a closet homosexual isn't very high. Otherwise, he would have sought a male dom and not a FEMDOM.

Later on, we're going to be revisiting sissy play at a more advanced level. For now, keep things relatively simple by letting him explore his feminine side.

## Pet Play

Role plays are quite common in dom-sub relationships. Some are rather "traditional," such as patient and doctor. However, FEMDOM is all about taking things a step further. One such role play that takes things to another level is pet play.

In this tactic, your sub is your pet. You can choose to make him an animal pet, or just a "human pet." Now, keep in mind that you are essentially reducing him to an animal. So, he can't think for himself. He needs to be given commands just like you would a dog, for instance. As such, he cannot do anything at all. He must be obedient to your every command.

This tactic is essentially meant to be a training tool. However, you can use it as part of foreplay if you wish. You can have him run around like your pet, perhaps with a leash around his neck, which can then lead to some type of sexual activity, such as performing oral on you. If he is a good boy, he might be able to get a treat, such as watching you masturbate or touch himself.

Other variations of pet play include riding him like a pony. While the point is not to actually ride him like a pony, what you achieve with this is to assert a dominant position over him. Consequently, he will get the idea that you are "on top"; hence you are the mistress.

Another great idea is to give him a pet name. Now, we don't mean things like "sugar" or "honey baby." We mean real pet names like "marbles" or "fuzzy." Using pet names can be a fun part of humiliation tactics. In such cases, the names you call him are meant to humiliate him without actually demeaning him.

## Treating Him Like a Child

There are some men who have severe mommy issues. As such, they like to be treated like children, or even babies for that matter. One interesting fetish that some guys have is being breastfed. Others like to dress up in diapers and prance around like babies. Some will even go as far as ask to have their diapers changed and get their bottle.

This particular tactic really depends on you. If you like, you can use it in combination with other tactics. For instance, if he is a good boy and serves you properly, you can breastfeed him is that is what he likes. Another interesting variation is a mother-son role play. For some guys, getting it on with mommy is the ultimate fantasy. But since they are subs, they need to do everything mommy says. Otherwise, they can't get what they want.

Not all FEMDOMS are into this kind of role play, but if you are up for it, it's definitely worth giving it a chance. Not all FEMDOMS like the idea of mothering their subs, but it might end up creating an interesting dynamic for both of you.

## Making Basic Tactics Work Effectively

The tactics which we have discussed in this chapter as pretty beginner-friendly. They don't require a great deal of sacrifice and are suited just fine for the novice sub. If you are not very experienced as a FEMDOM, it's also a good way for you to gauge what you want out of a relationship. Please keep in mind that subs don't need to know how experienced you are. But it certainly helps too if you know what you're doing.

In the event that you are in a committed relationship with your man and you are both exploring this kind of relationship, then you can both explore these tactics together. This will enable you to develop your own dynamic, as a couple, without having to consider any possible third parties. This type of journey can really bring you together as a couple and solidify your relationship. In addition, quite a few male subs have a hard time asking for it. They may hint at it through their actions and attitude but may never actually come out and say it.

Also, if you are contemplating having multiple subs, then these tactics will be essential in building the type of relationship you want with each of your subs. You can tweak them to suit your individual needs and the various personalities of your subs. Ultimately, you need to figure out what works best for you. That way, you can provide your subs with the guidance they need in order to fulfill your wishes.

Lastly, please keep in mind that this is a learning process. As you embrace your inner FEMDOM, you too, will begin to discover what turns you on the most. It could be something as simple as being served, or it could expand into something much larger such as BDSM.

In reality, it's all up to you!

In this world of FEMDOM, no one is here to tell you what to do. You are the mistress of your domain. And even if you decided to team up with other FEMDOMS to make a large event, there is no one who can tell you what to do. Your sub is your sub, and that's the end of it. You have the right to do whatever you want. After all, your sub is with you because they want to. You are not forcing them to be with you through brainwashing or anything like that. As such, you have every right to be who you want to be. It's your domain.

# Chapter 6: The Use of Physical Aggression in FEMDOM

Some form of violence is generally involved in dom-sub relationships. The level of violence depends on what both parties agree to. If violence, such as physical aggression, is utilized without the full consent of both parties, then essentially what you have is assault. In such cases, the victim needs to leave the relationship at once. If there is serious harm committed, then charges may have to be pressed.

That being said, the use of physical aggression can be a wonderful tool to assert your dominance over your mal sub. In fact, it is especially powerful as men are considered to be physically superior to women. As such, the act of having a woman physically hit a man is more powerful psychologically than it is physically. You don't need to beat your man to a bloody pulp in order for him to get the point. If anything, the threat of aggression is enough to render him helpless.

If that seems unbelievable, then you have seen nothing yet.

In this chapter, we are going to explore how the use of physical aggression can help you assert your position as a FEMDOM. Since we are still in a "training phase" so to speak, we are not going to look at physical aggression in bondage. This is something that we will be exploring later on. For now, we are going to focus on how you can use this tactic as a means of laying down the ground rules for your FEMDOM relationship.

## Using Your Hands to Assert Your Dominance

The level of force used in FEMDOM relationships largely depends on how much your sub is willing to tolerate without it becoming physical assault. Generally speaking, most male subs tolerate spanking, slaps in the face, or squeezing of the genitals (this is a torture technique we will look at later on). We don't advise you to kick your sub, especially when they are on the ground, as this could be potentially dangerous. Now, it's a completely different story if you place the soles of your feet on their back. This is more of a dominant gesture than aggression as such. Also, please refrain from punching as that may also cause serious harm, especially during the heat of the moment.

Now, it should be said that some men actually enjoy being beaten. This appeals to the masochistic side of a sub. In fact, plenty of men find it exciting to be beaten and then engage in sexual activity. However, please bear in mind that you are the dom, and as such, need to ensure your sub's wellbeing.

Additionally, please bear in mind that your sub will generally be in a vulnerable position. They may be on the floor, bound, or blindfolded. So, you want to make sure that they feel safe. Otherwise, the fear of actual bodily harm may end up spoiling the moment and turn you into a big bully.

So, don't be afraid to slap your man around. In doing so, he will learn his place, especially when he transgresses any of your rules. You man needs to know who's in charge, and you need to let him know that you run a tight ship. If he can't deal with it, then it's too bad for him. You're the boss, and you are going to make your presence felt.

## Using Artifacts to Assert Your Dominance

This is where it starts to get kinky. Devices such as floggers, whips, ropes, chains, and sticks are all used to hit subs. Many times, carrying a device around, such as a flogger, is mainly intended to be a display of power. The fact that you carry it around with you during sex play means that you are in charge. Furthermore, it is a great disciplining tool, especially when you are training a novice sub.

To use a flogger as a training aid, all you need to do is strike your sub every time they do something you don't like or if they do something wrong. For instance, if your sub does not address you properly, this would earn him a flogging in the back or butt (avoid flogging to the face as it could be quite dangerous). However, if the sub has done something right, it could earn him a tickling with the flogger as a reward.

Other devices, such as whips, are generally used as part of torture tactics. Yet, they could be used as a training aid, as well. Sticks come in various forms, sizes, and shapes. They can be used to both strike as well as poke your sub. Make sure you don't use sharp sticks to poke. However, poking can provide you a gentle nudge to your sub that they must do what they are expected.

As for ropes and chains, these are mainly used to restrain subs. Nevertheless, they could also be used to strike your sub. More than the actual pain ropes and chains can cause, it's the psychological impact that these devices have. After all, what good can come from being struck by a chain? Plus, chains are useful devices during pet play. You can walk your sub around like a dog, and if he misbehaves, a playful whack will serve as a kind reminder of what is expected of him.

## Kicking, Pushing, Wrestling and Other Kinds of Physical Aggression

For some guys, there is a rush in being dominated by a woman. This is quite common among larger women and smaller men. This type of situation creates arousal. There is something about being unable, or at least unwilling, to physically dominate a woman. Now, the average man has a greater brute physical force than the average woman. Yet, there are women who are substantially stronger than some men. It is this difference that makes men seek physically strong women.

As a matter of fact, it's quite tempting for female bodybuilders and exceptionally tall women to become dominatrices. Under such circumstances, it would be quite hard for a weaker man to put up any kind of resistance. This would constitute the ultimate turn on for a lot of guys.

However, you don't need to be physically superior to subject men through physical force. In fact, it's normal to see rather petite women engaging in the role of dominatrix without having to be physically superior. All they need to do is push the right buttons. For instance, having a good understanding of martial arts or self-defense can be enough to deter a man from trying to physically attack you. If they can see that you mean business, they won't try to put up a fight. They know that you can handle yourself.

Of course, not all FEMDOM relationships reach this point. However, it can be an interesting angle to pursue should it come to that point. Hey, if you're a bigger gal, you might even be able to manhandle a puny guy. He would love that, and you certainly would get a kick out it!

## Spanking and Genitals

Let's take things up a notch here. For some guys, getting hit in the genitals can be a turn on. In a manner of speaking, it's pleasure through pain. While getting nailed in the nutsack can be painful, when it's part of a FEMDOM dynamic, it can produce a feeling of pleasure and release. Often, you will find that most guys don't have an erection while getting hit in the genital area, but there is a good deal of logic to it, causing arousal.

You see, any type of hitting, spanking, or slapping in the genital region causes increased blood flow to this area. As a result, it is a good way of stimulating the blood that feeds the penis. This, in turn, promotes a strong erection.

This is a good technique to use, especially if you want your sub to penetrate you, but he might be having a bit of trouble getting things along. But keep in mind that we're not talking about some gentle tapping, here. We're talking about doing it hard enough to where he can wince in pain.

Additionally, genital spanking can be used as a punishment. To do this, a flogger, or perhaps a paddle, can be used. If your sub doesn't do as he is ordered, a nice tap in the genital area can be used to remind him of his duties.

However, there is one word of caution, though: the genital area can be quite sensitive. So, make sure that you don't go overboard and injure your sub. While you would have to strike him pretty hard, things can get out of hand in the heat of the moment. So, it's best to make sure that you don't overdo it. Otherwise, you may leave your man incapacitated (at least in that region) for a while. Plus, blunt force trauma in the genital region could lead to health issues. That's why it's best to take it easy.

Beyond that, your man should know that you are not afraid to resort to physical punishment if he is unable to live up to expectations. He needs to understand what your expectations are, and if he can't perform up to your standards, then there will be consequences.

## Physical Punishment

Okay, so now we're getting serious about punishing your man. While you may use psychological means of punishing your man, such as withholding gratification, insulting, name-calling, and perhaps sissy play, there needs to be some sort of physical punishment that you can use to assert your dominance.

In this regard, spanking is not the only thing you can do. While spanking (or any other type of physical aggression can be used), the truth is that there are other creative, less violent ways to make your man get the message. These tactics can be humiliating, or just play physically exhausting.

So, here are a couple of ideas.

First, make your man carry something heavy. A good trick is a bag full of pennies. Pennies, or any coins of that matter, can be quite heavy. Now, while the average guy would be able to pick them up easily, it's no so easy to hold a bag of pennies for a long time. This tactic works by having your sub extend his arms while holding a bag on pennies in each hand. After a few minutes, his arms will begin to tire. At this time, he cannot let go of the bag until you authorize him to do so. If he drops the bag, then he must not only pick it up but may be subject to additional punishment. You could spank him, or even humiliate him. After all, shouldn't a man be strong enough to hold a bag full of pennies? Additional ideas are a stack of books, dumbbells, or any other heavy object which he can hold in one hand.

Next, a great idea is to have your sub kneel on a pencil. That might not sound like such a bad thing. But after a few minutes of kneeling on a pencil, the pain can be nothing short of agony. To make things fun, he could kneel on a pencil while giving you oral pleasure. The punishment can end when you orgasm. If that takes a while... then too bad for him!

Lastly, why not make your man drop and give you 20? If he isn't very physically fit, it'll be tough for him to do 20 pushups in one go. If he can't do it, then further punishment may ensue. If you have a military streak about you, pushups, jumping jacks, or any other kind of physical exercise can be used as a punishment. This tactic is actually more of a reward as he would actually get in shape!

As you can see, physical aggression is more about causing a psychological impact on your sub rather than actually physically harming him. So, don't hold back and be creative. Just make sure not to go too far... at least for now!

# Chapter 7: Dressing Up for FEMDOM

Clothing is just as important as any other part of the FEMDOM dynamic. Typically, images of leather-clad women with whips come to mind. On the flip side, you see mean dressed in ass-less chaps while wearing a leather mask.

However, the truth is that dressing up for FEMDOM is about whatever you want it to be. You don't have to dress in a latex dominatrix suit to be a badass dom. After all, this may not be your style. The best way to go about clothing is to choose whatever makes you feel comfortable. This is about what makes you happy. Along the way, you might get some requests from your subs. This is important as FEMDOMS, who have multiple subs, may either choose to have on style across the board or perhaps dress in different styles to suit the fantasy the sub wants to be a part of.

This opens up two possibilities.

First of all, you are a FEMDOM, you have a style, and anyone that wants to be with you has to get with the program.

Fair enough.

Please keep in mind that you are a dom. You don't have to justify your style to anyone. If anything, subs need to explain themselves to you. They need to convince you to accept them in your life. Otherwise, you can kindly reject being with a sub simply because he doesn't suit your style.

For example, you could be the leather-clad type that has whips, floggers, and chains. While this is a more stereotypical BDSM set up, it's what a lot of guys want to experience. So, you can deliver that experience to them while satisfying your own power streak.

Also, you could be more into the mothering role. So, you would present yourself as a mother. This might imply babying your subs so that they are completely dependent on you. This may include activities such as diaper changing, breastfeeding, and treating your sub like an infant.

Another interesting twist is going goth. The whole dungeon set up can be quite exhilarating for some guys. They would rather get it on with a goth dungeon mistress than with a latex-clad dominatrix. While the dynamic might essentially be the same, the visuals and the can vary.

The second possibility can be found in a committed relationship. Let's assume that you and your partner are looking to explore the FEMDOM dynamic. So, you might end up having multiple roles that you can play. Perhaps your man wants to experience a doctor-patient environment. Or, he wants to be babied. In addition, he might be into the whole dungeon setup.

Now, it should be noted that you are not pleasing him. If he wants to be babied, then he has to earn that privilege. He needs to pay his dues before you can satisfy his mommy fantasies. If he wants to go into the dungeon, then he needs to pay his mistress respect before he can have the privilege of being accepted into the dungeon.

In this arrangement, the FEMDOM dynamic is fully under your control. The only thing different is that you are giving you male sub an incentive, something to look forward to, in a manner of speaking. He knows that if he is perfectly compliant, he will get to experience the situation that he longs for. Simply because he gets the chance to be who he wants to be, he will go along with whatever games you want to play with him.

It should also be said that mixing things up a bit is always fun. Perhaps you're not always in the mood for the dungeon. Perhaps you are in the mood to be the boss who takes advantage of her employees. Maybe you want to become a police officer that humiliates a criminal. Or you might be in the mood to be a military drill instructor who puts her new recruits through the wringer.

All of these scenarios are mere examples of the plethora of possibilities you can explore. However, whatever scenario you explore, they need to be set up in such a way that you retain control while making your sub earn his right to be a part of it. If you allow him to feel like you are giving him what he wants, then you are giving away your power. If he has willingly accepted to give his power away to you, then there is no reason why you should do anything to surrender an iota of it.

# Choosing the Right Dress for Your Sub

Choosing the proper outfit for your sub largely depends on your style. Generally speaking, most FEMDOMS have a number of different outfits their subs are expected to wear throughout their time under her command. This also depends on the type of game you want to play.

Let's consider this situation.

You have a new sub in your life. As such, he is automatically assigned to the lowest possible rank. This implies that he can expect nothing more than to be treated as the lowest piece of dirt (well, that's just us getting carried away a bit). So, he also needs to dress the part.

Now, you could just have him running around naked. That's pretty harsh on a new sub. It makes them feel vulnerable and weak. Psychologically, being naked exposes you so much that you don't really have a sense of power. In a way, you are already breaking his will.

Let's assume now that while you are "breaking in" your new sub, you want to have some pet play. Well, why not have "fluffy" or "fifi" wear a dog collar? Alternatively, he could wear a saddle so you can ride him. If you really wanted to ramp it up, there are butt plugs that have a tail on the end. Using this type of device serves both a practical purpose (anal play) and a psychological purpose (the animal tail). Plus, if it's a cute foxtail or something, it adds a sissy component to it.

As you can see, it's really a question of being creative!

Perhaps the only restriction to keep in mind is anything that would be degrading on the basis of cultural or religious reasons. Beyond that, there really shouldn't be any kind of restriction in your dress ideas. After all, he's your sub and has to get with the program.

## Costumes and Role Plays

This is a very common situation that arises in the FEMDOM world. When you get into role plays, you would naturally think about using costumes as a part of the scene. This is perfectly natural. After all, what would a good role play be without the use of costumes?

However, if you are so inclined to use costumes, there are a couple of things to keep in mind.

Firstly, what do you want to achieve? That is, your role is to dominate him. Therefore, costumes and role plays are not about what he wants. It's about what you want. So, it doesn't matter if he likes seeing you in any given outfit. If you don't want to wear it, there is no reason why you should.

Secondly, it's all about domination, right? So, wearing outfits that don't assert your dominance is not necessarily the best way to go.

Think about this situation.

Your sub may think you are looking absolutely smoking in a schoolgirl outfit, but how does that assert your dominance over him? That's the type of question you need to be asking yourself. Moreover, how does the costume fit into the overall powerplay you are seeking to make? If the costume does not contribute to asserting your position of power, then there is no reason for you to wear it

Lastly, any costumes your sub wears should not give him any power whatsoever. If anything, his costumes should reaffirm his submissive nature. So, if you are going to be a police officer, a prisoner outfit might be the best way to go. But if you are going to pretend to be a sexy cop and he's the big bad thief, then that is not really going to work out in your favor.

Costumes can also be used to humiliate your subs. If your sub likes dressing up in women's clothing, perhaps giving him a total girly outfit would provide him with the ultimate experience. Combine that with humiliating treatment, and you might have yourself one heck of a session. The main point here is to do anything, and everything you can, to show that you're the boss.

No questions asked.

## Common FEMDOM Dress Up Ideas

What you choose to wear should make you feel as comfortable as possible. It should be about you feeling good about yourself while also making you feel sexy.

There's nothing worse than wearing something that doesn't necessarily flatter you. Nevertheless, there are some universal looks that will never go wrong in the world of FEMDOM.

So, let's take a look at some of the classic items you can wear during your FEMDOM sessions.

- Knee-high or thigh-high boots. These are classics. They look great and assert a position of power. The high-heel boots really make a statement, especially if you want to degrade your man by stepping on him. They come in different colors, so these can be used in a variety of situations.

- Latex suits. Latex suits are practically a cliché in the FEMDOM and BDSM world. Still, they are timeless and serve to really drive your point home. Plus, most men fantasize about this type of outfit. So, it would certainly be worth giving it a go. Just make sure you are not allergic to latex.

- Anything that's leather. This is another classic style. Black leather is the industry standard though varying colors can also create an interesting combination of visuals. Red and white are very common colors and stand out very well in a dark setting.

- Lingerie. This is a bit tricky. If you wear lingerie, such as bodysuits or thongs, it is because you want to. This isn't meant to be a treat for him. Of course, he will be turned on by the fact that you look good, but that's just an added bonus for him. As far as you're concerned, you're not catering to what he likes. This is about what you like, and that's that.

- Corsets. Corsets are a staple of FEMDOM. They look good, and they are practical to wear. They allow you a free range of motion. This is important, especially if you are going to be engaging in bondage or any other type of physical activity. If you would rather have something looser on your body, a bustier might be a good option. Again, it looks good and provides you with the range of motion you would be looking for.

- Bodycon dress. These dresses have become very popular in recent years. They not only flatter your figure, but they also create the visual effect you want. Combining a bodycon with boots or stiletto heels creates the ultimate male fantasy.

- High heels. On the subject of heels, stilettos are another staple of FEMDOM. They create a wonderful image and go well with virtually any type of outfit. Stilettos work really well with skirts and dresses. However, if you choose to wear leather or latex pants, they can also complement your outfit very well.

- Stockings. These are a great complement to any outfit. Stockings are definitely sexy and are always in style. You will never go wrong with stockings. Fishnets work really well too. Plus, if you choose to undress, wearing stockings creates an interesting visual.

At the end of the day, whatever you choose to wear ought to make you feel comfortable and secure about yourself. The last thing you want is to go for a look that isn't you. Please remember that you don't have to look a certain way to be a knock-out FEMDOM. Your sub will go wild in anything you wear. So, don't hold back. This is your time to feel empowered.

# Chapter 8: Setting the Stage

FEMDOM is all about the ambiance that surrounds the practices you want to engage in. So, setting the scene is an important aspect as creating an environment that can assert your dominance is key. What that scene looks like is entirely up to you.

When going about setting the scene for your FEMDOM encounters, you must consider what you want to get out of it. This means that you must consider the way in which you wish to assert your dominance. One classic example is the dungeon motif. This scenario is conducive to pulverizing your subs if they choose to enter.

However, it's not always entirely possible to have your own dungeon. This is especially true if you don't have a place devoted exclusively to your encounters, and you have a house full of kids. Still, that doesn't mean you can't set things up just the way you like them.

That's why this chapter is focused on setting the stage for your encounters in such a way that you won't have any trouble making a considerable impression on your subs. Most importantly, it can become the type of scenario you enjoy most. This is the kind of situation in which you can feel comfortable, thereby giving you the greatest amount of pleasure.

## Privacy Is Key

Perhaps the biggest concern for FEMDOMS (and their subs, especially) is privacy. When you think about this aspect, it's important that you consider the need for a space that is away from prying eyes. This opens up a number of possibilities which you ought to consider.

First of all, does your current place of residence offer the option of setting up a room devoted exclusively to your escapes? Perhaps a basement or an extra bedroom could do the trick. This is particularly important if you're into the whole BDSM or dungeon setup. Thus, privacy becomes an important consideration.

There are other alternatives if you can't devote a specific place to your FEMDOM tactics. Lots of couples rent out hotel rooms. And while hotel rooms can't be easily converted into a dungeon, at least it provides a reasonable amount of privacy. Please keep in mind that just about every male sub is not keen on being publicly recognized as a sub. They may have no issue with being your sub, but they may have issues with everyone at the office knowing about it.

Also, renting out an apartment solely for the purpose of your encounters is also an option. However, this could be an expensive arrangement, although there is one alternative here. There are men who are willing to pay for the experience of being dominated. Now, this doesn't mean paying for sex by any means. There are guys who are perfectly willing to pay for a dominatrix to pound them. As strange as that may sound, there are plenty of guys who just want the experience of being manhandled by a woman. It may sound paradoxical, but they are not necessarily interested in the sexual experience. After all, you can decide to let them engage in sexual activity or not. In the end, it's your decision to pursue this avenue.

## Creating the Fight Environment

The whole dungeon motif is practically cliché in the world of FEMDOM. In addition, it should be noted that not all guys who seek the FEMDOM experience have the dungeon in mind. What they really want is the domination that comes from being reduced to dust by a dom.

So, this implies that your environment doesn't have to be converted into a torture chamber. You can outfit them with the toys and devices that you plan to use. In fact, there are many couples who carry out their FEMDOM dynamic is a regular apartment. There are instances where you find a leather-clad FEMDOM sitting in an armchair getting a pedicure from her pet sub.

What this means is that you don't need to have your house renovated to suit your FEMDOM preferences. Other couples who are in committed relationships make tweaks to their bedroom to suit their activities. For instance, they install heavy curtains to ensure privacy while arranging furniture to suit the types of activities they engage in. This may include keeping a closet, or chest, readily available (this is where the goodies can be hidden).

Another important consideration is sound. Lots of couples make sure that they are at liberty to make as much noise as they please. This not only applies to other household members, but also to the neighbors. After all, you don't want the neighbors to overhear what's going on...

As for lighting, this is also an important part of setting the stage. Plenty of couples prefer a darker environment. So, they might go ahead and install dimmers or even colored lightbulbs. Again, these types of tweaks enable you to set the mood just the way you like it.

With regard to scents, this aspect should ideally reflect what you like. Perhaps there are certain scents that please you. Or, you might be inclined to use foul smells, especially as part of humiliation tactics. Ultimately, it really depends on what you want to achieve with your experience.

Lastly, it's important to consider other people who may participate in your escapes. For instance, if you plan to engage in cuckoldry, you might want to make allowances for an additional person in your space. If you also plan to have multiple subs at the same time, then you should also keep those spatial considerations in mind.

At the end of the day, setting the scene largely depends on each person's circumstances. If you have the money and room to create your own dungeon, then by all means. But if all you want is a private area in which you can let your imagination fly, then there are plenty of minor tweaks you can make to suit your personal needs and style.

## What About Props?

This is a common concern when it comes to setting up your personal space. Many FEMDOMS use props in their encounters. This includes whips, chains, handcuffs, and so on. So, if you happen to use a good number of props, what do you do with them?

Now, if you have a dedicated space for them, then there's really no issue. You can just keep them in the same spot. That way, you won't have to search for them when you actually need them. Things get a bit trickier when you don't have a dedicated space.

Earlier, we mentioned keeping them in a closet or a chest. However, you may not be keen on spending time on setting things up before and organizing after every session. But don't worry, there are alternatives.

The most common storage solution is a "toy box." These boxes are disguised to look like a closet or a footlocker. They come in various sizes and can hold the toys and props you wish to use in your encounters. Plus, they are an inexpensive solution as they can be accommodated inside a closet or kept under the bed. The best thing about these boxes is that they don't take up a lot of space.

Another interesting storage alternative is a suitcase. These come in all sizes. They are great because you can travel with them as well. They can fit the number of toys and props you need while keeping them handy. This is important as you may not always have time to set up every prop you plan to use. In addition, if you get creative, your toys will always be on hand. That's what makes these types of suitcases so convenient.

Also, there are cloth rolls which you can use to store essential toys. These rolls look like the ones used by old-school doctors. When you unroll them, all of your toys or torture devices are revealed. They are great if you are not packing a lot, or just want the essentials on hand. Additionally, they are great if you are just starting out and don't have a lot of props, yet. They are easy to store and give you the option of carrying stuff around with you should scenes be carried out in various locations.

## All About Furniture

This is where things get really interesting.

If you the option of setting up a dedicated space for your FEMDOM scenes, then there are a number of options from which you can choose your furniture. The most common is just a plain table with stirrups or straps. These tables are plain wood though we would recommend going with stainless steel, kind of like surgical tables, just in case there are bodily fluids expelled at any point in time.

Having a dedicated table can help you with torture tactics. As a matter of fact, some gals like to set up their place to look like a workshop. So, the place a table in the middle with shelves and hooks holding up all the goodies. This type of setup doesn't exactly look like a dungeon. If anything, it looks like something taken out of a horror movie. But, if you're into it, then it certainly works for a terrifying experience.

Another very interesting piece of furniture you can use looks like a dentist's chair. You'll find them under the name of "facesit" chair. They are designed so that you can sit on your sub's face while they lie down. While the chair isn't exactly designed with your sub's comfort in mind, it's intended to avoid suffocation. It can also be used as means of torture as it gives you access to your sub's lower body without them being able to see what you are doing.

You will also find a chair that resembles a regular chair, like the kind you would have in your dining room, but without the bottom. This chair is generally used for torture tactics. The sub sits in this chair, usually bound or restrained so that the genital area is exposed. This type of chair is used in cock and ball torture, or just for the purpose of giving a couple of friendly whips.

Lastly, you will find an assortment of couches and sofas, which can also be used as part of your FEMDOM tactics. Of course, you can use a regular couch, in particular, the armrests, to bend over your sub. However, one popular type of sofa-like piece of furniture looks like an "m." This is used to bend the sub over. It's great for penetration, such as with a dildo or strap-on, and also allows for restraint. It is also a fun place to sit and relax if you should so choose.

## A Word of Caution

Perhaps the biggest mistake when starting out with FEMDOM is rushing out to get a bunch of things. The fact is that it's always best to refrain from making significant purchases at first. The reason for this is that you might get stuff that doesn't really go with your persona. This is why it's always recommended to purchase your gear as you find your identity in the FEMDOM world.

For example, you might be gung-ho about the whole dungeon setup but then realize it's not really you. So, you end up spending a bunch of money on a number of things which don't really suit your style. On the contrary, you can experiment with various things and move on from there.

One simple idea is to get an old chair from a garage sale or thrift store, cut out the bottom and use that as a facesit chair. You don't spend a great deal of money, and you are able to experiment with something specific. In anything, it's probably best to get old furniture as your subs may end up having bathroom accidents while on the chair. So, you don't want a nice piece of new furniture being spoiled.

On the whole, you can turn any space into your personal lair. All you need is to find your identity and take it from there!

# Chapter 9: Accessories... Accessories... Accessories...

Throughout this book, we have mentioned toys, accessories, and other goodies. So, the time has come to drill down and focus on what these toys are and how you can use them in your FEMDOM scenes. The main thing here is to look at the array of options and then choose the ones that suit your preferences best.

Now, it should be noted that there are all kinds of kinky toys out there. Some of them look like they were pulled out of a medieval torture chamber. Others are just plain and straightforward stuff you see in movies. Ultimately, it depends on how far you want to take things and how much you want to push your subs.

It should also be said that you don't really need toys to make your presence as a FEMDOM felt. In fact, there are FEMDOMS out there who make a name for themselves by using household stuff. That can add a really mind-bending dimension to your games.

In this chapter, we are going to focus on the main types of toys that you can use and how they can be implemented to really get the most out of your FEMDOM role plays.

## Whips, Ropes, and Chains

These artifacts are typical of BDSM. They are used to restrain subs while also inflict pain upon them. Of course, we're not talking about torturing people to death. We are making a point though of how you can use these artifacts to give your subs the experience they have been looking for.

First off, whips are quite common. They are used in a plethora of situations. Most commonly, they are used to discipline subs. When a sub gets out of line, cracking the whip becomes a must. Whips are also one of the staples in the dungeon or goth setup. They are cool and can really create the effect you are looking for.

Also, the use of floggers is common. For most FEMDOMS, some kind of combination of whips or floggers gives them control over their subs. This is especially important when you think about how much subs relish in their pain. Plus, it's a relatively harmless way of giving subs what they deserve.

Now, here's a good way in which you can subject your subs to some kinky pain. Sit your sub on the bottomless chair. You can use a rope to restrain them, or perhaps a chain for greater effect. Now, take the whip or flogger, and hit them under the chair. This will land the blow right on the testicles. The pain that this tactic causes can be quite considerable. The only thing to be careful with here is to avoid hitting them too hard. A good rule of thumb is to start off easy and ramp it up as much as the sub can take it. The use of a safe word would come in handy here if you should so choose.

In addition, using handcuffs is useful when looking to keep your sub from moving about. Police handcuffs work well though you need to be careful you don't lose the key. Alternatively, shackles can create a seriously mind-bending experience. The leather shackles seem to work best as they won't purposely damage your sub's wrists. However, you might have subs who are into the full-blown experience. If that's the case, then why not indulge your sub?

## All About Masks

We could write an entire book about masks!

Seriously, masks play such a prominent role in BDSM, FEMDOM, and dungeon scenes. The main attractiveness to them is that masks offer a degree of anonymity to both sub and mistress. Mainly, it allows subs to feel even more submissive as they are reduced to a faceless element.

As for the mistress (or master in any event), it allows for a psychological effect based on the power dynamic that you have chosen. Some FEMDOMS would rather not wear a mask and simply go for gothic makeup. Some FEMDOMS won't wear anything at all. As always, it's a question of what you prefer.

First off, there are masks that are intended to block the sub's visuals. These masks may resemble blindfolds or sleeping masks. They don't do much in the way of fomenting submission but can be a good means of getting newbies to settle in.

Then, there are full-face coverings. The classic mask is the one with the zipper for a mouth. If you search for a "gimp" mask, you will find an array of full-face coverings that resemble medical face masks, military gas masks, or the kind that have the zipper for a mouth.

These masks are used to indicate silence. As such, the sub has no means of uttering a sound. In the event that subs cry out in pain, these masks muffle sounds. So, they also serve this purpose. However, care needs to be taken that the sub does not suffocate. This can become an issue, especially if they are restrained.

That's why it's best to check to make sure your sub can breathe alright.

There are other types of masks that are basically animal faces. These are used in humiliation tactics. For instance, you are treating your sub like the animal that they are. So, it is only fitting that they actually look the part.

As for military gas masks, some FEMDOMS and BDSM practitioners are into the whole Nazi setup. So, the old-style WWI gas masks add a touch of horror to the entire situation. For example, the FEMDOM can wear one to create a scene of panic while the sub may wear a plain full-face covering. Another twist is a surgical face mask that makes it seem like the FEMDOM is a demented doctor. The sub has no choice but to swallow their fear.

Please note that there is a myriad of masks to choose from. So, it really depends on what you like and what you feel is fitting for your sub(s).

## Dildos and Strap-ons

Now we're talking about anal play. This is big-league stuff for most guys. While new subs may not be into this much, at least not right away, you will find that most subs are actually yearning for some kind of anal play. As such, you can use these artifacts to your advantage.

Let's start with dildos. There are many kinds of dildos out there. You can find some really creative ones while others that are out of a horror film. However, when it comes to male subs, dildos don't really need to be creative. They just need to get the job done.

For most subs, though, they may have very little anal play experience. So, you might want to ease them a little bit. To this end, butt plugs may serve best. Butt plugs are shorter and are built to facilitate penetration. They are made out of glass or rubber. If your sub is completely new to anal play, a rubber butt plug might be your best choice.

Butt plugs are very useful when training your sub as you can require them to have one inserted throughout your time. Stricter mistresses require subs to wear them throughout their regular day. If your sub is compliant with this, then you may have yourself a fully trained butt slave in short order.

As for dildos, glass dildos may not be your best choice with inexperienced subs. You might want to try rubber ones as they provide the easiest experience. They come in all shapes and sizes. So, having a couple in different lengths and circumferences can help create an interesting experience for your sub.

Also, vibrators can work well, too. While they don't create the same effect as they do in women, vibrators can offer a different kind of sensation for your sub. You will find that your subs will gladly accept dildos as part of their training at one point or another.

When it comes to strap-ons, you will find these to be the ultimate power rush. When you have a sub, who is bent over and practically helpless, penetrating them can provide you with a rush of adrenaline while the sub learns his place. Like dildos, strap-ons come in all shapes and sizes. So, you can choose the one that best suits your preferences.

Additionally, anal beads are quite popular when training subs. These are a bit uncomfortable at first but can provide you with the training your subs need if you are planning to go deep with them. They come in various sizes. So, you can start off with a smaller size and work your way up.

## Trying Out All Kinds of Goodies

In the world of FEMDOM, there are all kinds of goodies you can try out. These all depend on how far you plan to take things and what your subs can tolerate. There are cases in which your subs can only take so much. So, it's a good idea to go easy on them. In other cases, your subs might be able to handle a lot more. That can be your cue to really turn up the heat.

One goodie you might want to try is the cock ring. These rings are placed around the penis when it is flaccid. Then, as the penis grows in size, the ring constricts around the penis. This makes it painful to get an erection. This forces the sub to cool it. Similarly, ball rings constrict the testicles. This creates an overall sensation of pain while cutting off circulation. These are used as a common torture tactic.

Ball gags are also used during kinky play. They can be an interesting alternative to masks. There are ball gags that give the sub something to bite down on or just a regular gag, which is meant to both muffle sound and restrict breathing. Care needs to be taken with these so that the sub doesn't suffocate during an encounter. It's always important to be sure your subs are safe as they fully trust you.

Clamps are also commonly used in BDSM and FEMDOM play. Clamps are usually placed in very sensitive areas such as the nipples, penis, or tongue. They are meant to cause pain while providing your sub with stimulation in certain areas. Placing clamps on testicles can be used as a torture tactic.

You will also find some extreme toys such as needles. Using sharp objects are truly extreme. We don't recommend the use of these types of torture tactics as they can put your sub's wellbeing in danger. The same goes for full-body latex suits. They can cause your sub to suffocate. As such, it's best to avoid using these types of devices until you are fully aware of what you are doing.

## Choosing the Right Toys for You

At the end of the day, choosing the right toys should be about finding the best ones to suit your individual tastes. If your sub is yearning for anal play, then, by all means, oblige him. This is why we have repeatedly stated that this is your domain. Any sub that chooses to enter must know what they are up against.

Consequently, they must deal with whatever you throw their way. This will not only help you assert your dominance but also give you the pleasure that comes with inflicting pain and torture on your subs.

So, do take the time to go over what's available on the market. Since it may be hard to choose, you might want to start out with the essentials and take it from there. Also, don't be shy about trying household items out. For instance, using an old electrical cord as a restraint is a weird but effective idea. Old paintbrushes are great for teasing while clothespins make fabulous clamps. As such, you don't need to spend a great deal of money to really spice things up. A little creativity can go a long way, especially when your subs are begging for more!

# Part III: Basic FEMDOM Tactics

# Chapter 10: Humiliation Tactics

Humiliation is a common tactic used in FEMDOM. Just about every kind of blog, book, or program you see about FEMDOM includes humiliation as its main focus. However, we are not going to focus this book solely on humiliation. In fact, it's just one of the tactics you can use to dominate your male subs.

Does that sound interesting?

Indeed, you can use humiliation as just one means of exerting your dominance. Most importantly, there are a number of various tactics that you can put into practice. So, it's not that there is just "humiliation." There is a number of ways in which you can put humiliation into practice. By following these tactics, you will surely drive your main point home.

## The Main Purpose of Humiliation

The main purpose behind humiliation is not to debase de human condition of your subs. This is something that perhaps gets lost with a lot of the websites and videos you find nowadays. The point of humiliation is to subjugate your subs to your command. As such, they need to understand who is in charge and what this represents to them, and to you. So, the use of humiliation tactics is intended to further break the sub into a submissive role.

Moreover, you can easily see how subs settle into a subservient role by the way the faithfully execute your orders and commands. Consequently, you don't need to denigrate your subs in order to get them fully immersed in a submissive role.

Additionally, humiliation tactics are quite broad. They can go from rather basic elements such as sissy play to more graphic situations like bathroom play. Ultimately, it's a question of seeing how much your sub can tolerate. If you find that they can handle their fair share of humiliation, then you can be certain that you will find a good balance between dominance and submission.

## Sissy Play

The first tactic we are going to look at is sissy play. Earlier, we talked about how sissy play is one of the first things that most subs experience. When you are looking to use it as part of humiliation, sissy play can be seen as a means of putting your sub into a deeply submissive role.

The first step to sissy play is cross-dressing. Some guys love to dress up in girls' clothes, or perhaps have a fetish about it. So, you are only too happy to oblige. With sissy play, you can use your imagination. For example, your subs can wear female panties while they prance around for your amusement. In other cases, they can wear makeup and dresses. Some cross-dressing play includes dressing up like a doll.

If you feel inclined, a gimp mask can add an interesting touch to your sub. If you wish to take photos to use as humiliation material later on, just make sure you don't capture your sub's face. The last thing you want is to have intimate photos leaking out. Nevertheless, using photos as humiliation material, later on, is quite useful. You can have your subs go through this humiliation and then use the photos as a means of blackmail if they should ever get out of line.

Another component of sissy play is anal play. With anal play, your sub is placed in the role of receiver. As such, you are treating them like a sissy because they secretly enjoy being penetrated. You can use dildos or strap-ons for this purpose. However, more extreme domination games include another male penetrating the sub. While this may be taking things a bit too far, you may be surprised to find your subs agreeing to this.

Lastly, sissy play is a psychological tactic in which roles are reversed. So, the FEMDOM takes on the traditional male role while the male sub takes on a traditional female role. Thus, your sub is well aware that they don't have much power while in your presence. This means they can either deal with it or get out.

## Shaming and Name-Calling

FEMDOMS love to assign pet names to their subs. Now, by "pet names," we don't mean "boo" and "honey." We mean things like naming your sub as you would a pet. This is important for two reasons. First, you avoid using your sub's real name, thereby ensuring discretion. Second, you are creating an alternate person for your sub. As such, they might be Mr. Smith, sales manager, out there in the real world, but inside your domain, they are "Fifi" or "meatball." This type of tactic ensures that subs are certain to remember who they are in your presence.

Also, name-calling extends to making specific references to their physical appearance. A chubby sub may be referred to as "fatso." Perhaps your thin sub might become "skinny" when being referred to. Again, the idea here is to force your sub to remember who they are at all times. Perhaps the only limit here would be to refrain from mocking a physical disability. Doing so would be downright mean. Although it really depends on the dynamic that you have. Still, it's best to avoid shaming a sub if they clearly have a disability.

That being said, shaming also extends to open chastising your subs for their behavior. For instance, you allow your sub to touch themselves while you torture them in some manner. As the play proceeds, the sub ejaculates. Consequently, you proceed to shame your sub for doing so. Some mistresses can be quite strict and shame their subs for even getting an erection without being told to do so.

Additionally, shaming can be used constantly as a means of reminding subs of their place. For example, if they are big and tall, you might use shaming like, "you're a big tall guy out there but nothing more than a sissy in here." This type of shaming has a practical, psychological effect on the sub. Therefore, the sub is reduced to a clearly submissive role.

Shaming is also commonly used when subs don't follow orders or don't meet expectations. Let's assume you command your sub to shave you. But they hurt you in some manner. Depending on your style, you can verbally lash out at your sub for nicking your skin. You can use all kinds of verbal jabs like "you're so useless" or "your absolutely worthless." While such statements would be completely cruel in the real world, bear in mind that this isn't the real world!

## Humiliation As Punishment

Another interesting angle is to use all of the tactics that we have mentioned earlier as a means of punishment. So, any of the tactics we have mentioned in this chapter can be used as a manner of disciplining your sub. Let's say that your sub doesn't particularly enjoy sissy play. Well, that's what they get if they don't live up to your expectations. Perhaps you can put a leash on them and take them around for a walk if they don't follow your orders to the letter.

Another punishment tactic is to use specific name-calling to remind the sub of their transgressions. When the sub messes up, a particular name is used. For example, you may not use an animal name during regular interaction. But as soon as your sub makes a mistake, then this name is used. A name such as "bobo" (you can come up with your own, for sure) would be used to remind the sub that they messed up, "you're useless bobo, aren't you?) this is a powerful humiliation tactic that can really drive a point home, especially when subs don't really seem to follow your orders.

Also, this is where you can bring out humiliating videos or photos. If your sub doesn't seem to get it, they can be reminded of the consequences unless they shape up. A powerful tactic is to take pictures or videos of them being penetrated. It can really drive the point home should they not follow your orders to your liking. Again, just make sure your sub's faces aren't visible. Trust us; it's best to play it safe with this kind of material.

## Cuckoldry

We saved the best for last.

Cuckoldry is derived from a medieval word that was used to denote men whose wives cheated on them with another man. The key here is that the man had some kind of knowledge about it but didn't do anything. This term was coined from birds who would raise another bird's eggs in their own nest. It was kind of like raising children that were not yours biologically. While being a stepparent is nothing to be ashamed of in human society, it is in the animal kingdom. Consequently, the term was used to denote men who were cheated on by their wives. During medieval times, a cuckold was generally the last guy to find out about it. The entire town knew who the cuckold was except the cuckold himself.

Translate that concept to our day and age, and you get a man whose wife (or committed partner) openly cheats on him with another man. Now, there is a difference between cuckoldry and swinging. Swinging implies consent among both parties. Also, swingers open exchange partners. This is the main difference with your average cuckold. The cuckold cannot have any other partners. They are forbidden to have another partner lest they incur the wrath of their mistress.

Now, let's take a look at the various dimensions of cuckoldry.

There is cuckoldry within a committed relationship, such as marriage or a long-term stable relationship. In this scenario, the mistress openly brings in other men with whom she engages in sexual intercourse. This is important as the humiliation increases in proportion as the mistress has sexual intercourse with the third party. It should be noted that the third party is not necessarily a sub. Otherwise, the cuckoldry scenario doesn't play out well. In fact, the mistress may have open displays of affection to the third man. Moreover, the mistress may even pleasure the man in order to increase the level of humiliation of the cuckold.

The most common level of cuckoldry is forcing the sub to watch. This is humiliation enough. However, humiliation can increase considerably. In order to further humiliate your sub, you can ask him to participate in the sexual act. For instance, the sub may be forced to masturbate the third man. This is particularly humiliating if the sub doesn't have any attraction toward other men.

Additionally, the sub can be humiliated by being the recipient of the third man's ejaculation. For instance, the third man may engage in sexual intercourse with the mistress and then ejaculate on the sub. Generally, the ejaculation is shot off on the sub's face. The sub may even be asked to swallow the semen.

Perhaps the ultimate level of cuckoldry is having the third man penetrate the sub. This can be done after being forced to watch the mistress engage in sexual activity with the third man. Naturally, this is especially humiliating for the sub, particularly if they are not attracted to men.

As you can see, cuckoldry is, in many ways, the ultimate form of humiliation. However, if you are not in a committed relationship with your subs, then you might find that the more extreme forms of cuckoldry are suitable. The use of masks might be your best option in order to ensure the privacy of all parts, especially if there is a video taken of the events. Nevertheless, cuckoldry can turn out to be the biggest power rush you can get in the FEMDOM world. Oh, and don't forget that cuckoldry is an effective means of punishment, especially if your sub decides to engage in sexual activity with someone other than you. So, if you are able to find willing participants, why not give it a chance? Subs who are not your committed partners will find it humiliating to be manhandled by another male while you are running the entire show!

# Chapter 11: Oral Play

What would FEMDOM be without some good oral play?

Now, please note that we are not talking about you, the FEMDOM, engaging in oral with your sub. That's the last thing your sub deserves. This is about your sub taking the time to please you orally. Therefore, you must make sure that your sub knows the rules of the game. Otherwise, there will be consequences to face.

Oral play is an essential part of the whole FEMDOM dynamic. It can be used as a part of your regular scenes while it can also be used as a form of humiliation. As such, it is quite versatile and provides FEMDOMS with any number of options to make their sub's life quite interesting.

In this chapter, we are going to explore the role of oral play in the FEMDOM world and how you can make the most of this fun experience for both you and your sub(s).

## Oral Play Fun

Oral play is commonly used to have the sub pleasure of the FEMDOM. This is really the only way you can really consider oral play to make sense within the FEMDOM domain. Now, you might perform oral on your sub, but as part of teasing torture (more on that in a bit).

So, things can get pretty wild from here.

Let's start with the basics. Firstly, you can have your sub perform oral on you by simply pleasuring you with their mouth. It's up to you if you would like to have your sub perform oral on you until you orgasm. Regardless, the sub is there to please you no matter what the circumstances.

When performing oral on you, you must command the sub so that he can perform it in the manner you prefer most. This could be through the use of the mouth, lips, and tongue. If you would like the sub to use their fingers, that could work, too.

One of the fun twists of this tactic is to have a whip or flogger. That way, you can direct your sub to do things as you like. This means that if the sub isn't meeting your expectations, you can give him a gentle nudge to remind him of the way you enjoy doing things.

Now, oral play is part of the FEMDOM power dynamic. Therefore, your sub must be in a position of inferiority. So, this generally positions the FEMDOM sitting on a bed, couch, or chair while the sub is generally kneeling. Earlier, we mentioned how kneeling on a pencil as a torture tactic. Well, this is a great moment to put that tactic into practice. If you take your sweet time enjoying the oral play, then the discomfort would be prolonged for the sub.

Also, you can break out your facesit chair. This is the perfect time to use it. You can comfortably sit in the chair while your sub takes care of business. As you can see, this is why facesit chairs are so popular. Alternatively, a bottomless chair can work just fine. The only issue here would be to make sure it's the right height. That way, your sub can do the business without making too much of a fuss.

You may choose to require your sub to use toys are part of oral play. If you are inclined to do so, then you must give your sub explicit instructions on how you wish them to use the toys you provide. Most commonly, subs are required to use vibrators in addition to performing oral play. In doing so, you must rid your sub of any restraints. At the very least, they would need to be able to use their hands. Please keep in mind that any use of toys is done with the sole purpose of pleasuring you. Don't think for a moment that your sub has the free rein to cause any kind of discomfort to you. This would be grounds for punishment. So, it's important that your sub is reminded of that.

## Oral Play Teasing Torture

You may want to use teasing as a means of torturing your sub. To achieve this, you can resort to oral play. Now, the last thing your sub can expect from you is for you to go out of your way to please him. That is why this teasing torture is all that more powerful. You are essentially giving your sub a glimmer of hope, yet you yank it away just as easily.

Oral teasing torture is generally used when the sub is bound. You can tie up your sub to a table or a chair.

Then, you can really turn up the heat. For this torture, a feather duster works really well. It is especially cruel if your sub has an erection. You can use the duster to tickle sensitive areas while giving him some dirty talk. You can make your sub beg you to touch them. Then, as you make it seem like you will be giving him oral pleasure, you can move away. Doing this multiple times can really drive your sub nuts. Some even ejaculate from the excitement. If that is the care, the shaming, name-calling, or some other type of punishment may ensure.

Some FEMDOMS may actually perform some kind of oral on their subs but generally when they are in a committed relationship. You can do this as a means of showing some kind of appreciation for your sub, who is also a life partner. In such cases, you might be inclined to give your sub a thrill or two.

## Oral Play Humiliation

This part is quite interesting and entertaining. Oral play can be used as a means of humiliating your sub, especially if you want to punish them. It's quite interesting to see how they react, particularly when asked to do something they are uncomfortable with.

One of the most common oral play humiliation tactics is to do oral on a dildo or strap-on. At first, it might seem a bit strange to your sub. After all, it's not that common to fool around like that with a dildo. However, the fact that it's shaped like a penis makes it psychologically intense. To take this exercise further, you can make your sub suck on the dildo or strap-on in order to lube it up prior to anal play. Then, the sub must suck on it to keep it lubed up so the anal play can continue.

This tactic can be taken further if you have multiple subs. One sub can suck on the dildo or strap-on, which is then inserted into another sub. It can make for a very intense experience, especially if you have brand-new subs.

Another interesting part of oral play humiliation is to have your subs lick your shoes and boots. Specifically, you can have your subs lick the soles of your footwear. This may not have any practical purpose as far as sex goes, but it serves quite well to create a strong effect of submission. This is quite commonly done when training new subs. So, do make sure to incorporate it as part of your new sub training regimen.

Also, for the foot fetish fans, subs can be required to kiss your feet, lick your soles or suck on your toes. Now, you might also ask them to paint your toenails, but that would be a fun little reward for them. So, if you, or your sub, happen to have a foot fetish, this is the way to go. You will find that many FEMDOMS make a point of having their subs perform oral play on their feet. While it's not quite humiliation (especially if they like it), it can be pretty rough if your sub isn't into feet. Additionally, you may require your subs to wash your feet, give you a pedicure, or just massage your feet after a long session of dominating subs.

If you are looking to take it up a notch, performing oral on another male is essentially the limit for a lot of subs. This exercise can be a part of cuckoldry or just plain humiliation.

In cuckoldry, the cuckold will most likely be required to perform oral play on the third male. While this is not always the case, it's generally part of the ultimate experience the cuckold is asked to go through. Should the cuckold refuse, then there may be physical punishment to be had. If the sub definitely refuses to go any further, then you may have to reconsider their commitment to being a sub.

When cuckolds perform oral on a third male, the cuckold may be required to receive the ejaculation from the third male or simply perform oral prior to, or after, the third man has penetrated you. Also, the cuckold can be required to perform oral play multiple times throughout penetration. One other angle is to have the cuckold lick the third male's testicles while he is penetrating you.

In the event that you have multiple subs on board, they may be required to perform oral play on each other. However, you can limit just how much fun they have with each other. For instance, you may keep them from ejaculating, or you may require them to finish off the other sub. Some FEMDOMS use this tactic as a means of providing their subs release, especially if they have been subjected to teasing torture.

This tactic can be further enhanced by the use of masks. So, if a sub is unable to see the other sub on whom they are performing oral play, they may be less inclined to feel weird about it. At the same time, the lack of visuals can create a very eerie scenario for your subs.

And then, there is rimming. Rimming consists of performing oral play on the anal region of another person. As such, rimming offers a number of interesting alternatives. For starters, your sub may be asked to perform rimming on you. This can be done while you squat on his face or while sitting in a facesit chair. The sub can use the mouth or tongue to perform the rimming action.

Also, you can have subs rim one another, especially if you are prepping them for anal play. For instance, one sub may be asked to rim the other prior to your penetration of them with a dildo or strap-on. This works quite well in a group setting, especially when you are running a dungeon with multiple subs.

If you are engaging in cuckoldry, you can have the sub rim the third male either as part of the humiliation exercise or perhaps while he is penetrating you. In this case, the sub may be lying on his back while you squat over him in a reverse cowgirl position. This would leave the sub's face exposed to the third male's testicles and anus. You can even throw in some teasing torture just for good measure.

Lastly, oral play can lead to humiliation when you have your subs lick the floor or any other surface.

While this may seem unclean, well, your sub really has no choice. Of course, you are not going to ask him to lick the garage floor, but just having them lick the floor as part of their training is enough to set the tone for their experience. Some FEMDOMS like having their subs kiss the ground they walk on. It's a metaphorical way of forcing your subs to worship you as their mistress.

As you can see, oral play has many different facets to it. You can be as creative or as extreme as you like. We have explored many different ways in which oral play can become a part of your domination tactics. So, it's always good to start off easy and then ramp things up to the point where your subs can handle things. You'll be surprised to find your subs handling a lot more than you think!

# Chapter 12: Getting Messy

In FEMDOM and BDSM, "getting messy" can get, well, messy. By "messy," we're referring to bathroom play. Now, bathroom play can cover a lot of different areas. Generally speaking, bathroom play involves humiliating your sub(s). As such, you can take this as far as you want. This means that your subs may be in for quite a messy time.

It should be noted that bathroom play isn't for everyone. It's a very specific fetish that some people really enjoy while others would rather avoid it. Depending on your personal tastes, you may want to engage in it or not.

In this chapter, we are going to take a look at bathroom play, the various types of tactics you can employ within the realm of bathroom play.

## Bathroom Play 101

In essence, bathroom play can involve anything related to the bathroom and activities conducted in the bathroom. One of the simplest activities in engaging in sexual intercourse in the bathroom. But that would be something that regular couples would do. As such, FEMDOM takes things to a whole new level.

When looking at bathroom play, you are really going to test your tolerance levels. If you are squeamish, this may not be the best type of tactic for you. Yet, if you are not afraid of pushing the envelope, then by all means.

If you are really into pushing things to the extreme, you will find that "toilet slavery" is one of the most extreme activities you can enjoy. The main reason behind this is that it pushes the limits of your tolerance. Since we associate the bathroom with dirtiness, it can be quite hard to get over the psychological barrier pertaining to this. Consequently, you may find it hard to engage in bathroom play. Yet, as we have mentioned, this is a bit of a niche fetish. There are some subs who are perfectly willing to go along with it.

Now, one word of caution. Make sure you have the means to keep everything tidy when engaging in this type of play. The issue here is that if things get really messy, then cleaning up may get pretty rough afterward. Sure, your sub is there to do the dirty work, but you may end up with a bigger mess than you had bargained for.

## Golden Showers

One common bathroom fetish is known as "golden showers." In essence, "golden showers" refers to the FEMDOM urinating on her sub. This is primarily done as a humiliation tactic, though it can be used as a means of satisfying a fetish.

It should also be noted that golden showers differ from a squirting orgasm, that is when females urinate following an orgasm. These types of orgasms are common in porn films and are generally seen when the female is in a submissive role. In this case, golden showers are a means of showing dominance over a sub.

The most common practice is to have the FEMDOM simply urinate over the sub. This can be done by simply squatting over the sub, or by way of sitting in a bottomless chair. At this point, things can get really kinky.

Firstly, you can simply urinate over your sub's body. Really, anywhere on his body will do, although you may find that the chest area is the most common. The sub may be restrained in some form or simply lying down. In most cases, the sub is restrained in one manner or another.

Secondly, an even kinkier twist may include the FEMDOM urinating on the sub's face. The sub may be required to swallow or simply take the blast. Masks may or may not be used though they generally are. The sub is not usually allowed to wipe anything off. As such, they may be required to lie there in a pool of urine. This is why we recommend that you make sure cleaning up afterward doesn't pose a bigger problem.

Some fetishes involve drinking urine. For instance, the sub may be required to collect the urine in a container and then drink it. Also, the sub can be required to lick or perform oral play on the FEMDOM after urination, thereby licking off the excess urine.

As you can see, golden showers are part of a fetish, which may or may not be used as a humiliation tactic. Golden showers among subs are not commonly used, and it is not generally seen as a part of cuckoldry. Although, anything goes as long as all parties are involved.

## Scat/Toilet Play

Things get really messy here. Scat or toilet play (also know was "toilet slavery") involves feces. Like golden showers, subs are required to receive feces from their FEMDOM. When you think about this type of play, you really have to be open to anything. After all, you may not be entirely comfortable with defecating on your subs. Nevertheless, some subs relish in this type of play as it is one of the most extreme fetishes.

Basic scat play generally involves the FEMDOM defecating on the sub on any part of his body. The sub may be restrained in some manner, as is usually the case, though he may simply lie on the floor. The FEMDOM may defecate by squatting over the sub or use a bottomless chair. In some play, the sub may then be required to rub the feces all over his body. Pictures and videos of this can subsequently be used as a humiliation tactic, although it should be noted that most bathroom play involves the use of masks as a means of privacy.

To make things more extreme, the FEMDOM may defecate on the sub's face and mouth. This is really extreme as the feces may then be smeared over the sub's face. In a very kinky, and perhaps nasty twist, the sub may be asked to eat the feces. As such, the sub is "eating out" of his FEMDOM's ass.

Another twist to this fetish includes rimming the FEMDOM after defecation. Needless to say, the sub licks the feces from the FEMDOM's ass. This is certainly extreme and even repulsive to some. Again, it's a question of seeing how far your subs are willing to go.

This is why scat is a very specialized fetish. Not all FEMDOMS do it, but those who do may find some very loyal subs. Subs who have this particular fetish relish in having their FEMDOMS dominate them in this manner. So, it's worth considering if you are inclined to such messy tactics.

## Tips for Bathroom Play

As you can see, bathroom play can get pretty messy. After all, urinating and defecating on the floor can be quite tough to clean up. So, let's take a look at some helpful tips if you choose to engage in this type of play.

If you have a dedicated space, or room, such as a dungeon, you may be able to install a drain. This can really facilitate things as you can simply hose down the area afterward. This will avoid having to clean up and mop the floor. In particular, if you engage in scat, having feces on the floor is not a fun thing to clean up. Even if you get your sub to clean up after himself, it can still be a problem leaving the area neat and tidy.

Also, having a dedicated area can enable you to set up the gear you need, such as a facesit chair. This makes it easy to clean up should things get really messy. Otherwise, you may consider laying down a tarp beneath the chair to ensure that you have an easier time cleaning up afterward.

In cases where you don't have a dedicated space, some FEMDOMS prefer to use the bathroom itself. This can make sense as, well, that's what a bathroom is for. Some like to use a bathtub as it is quite easy to clean up after. Also, the bathroom floor is also equipped to handle such messes. So, you might find t easier to just go ahead and carry out your play right on the bathroom floor.

If you plan to do bathroom play in a hotel, stick to the bathroom. The last thing you want to do is make a huge mess in a hotel room. If you do, you might get nailed with extra charges for cleanup. Needless to say, that's not the best way to go about it. So, sticking to the bathroom is usually a good choice.

It's also important to have a shower available. Smells can get on pretty strong. So, it would be nice if all those involved had a chance to shower. You can make a game of it. If your sub wants to shower afterward, he will have to earn it. For instance, you could have him shave you while in the shower. Also, you could have him give you a bubble bath. You can always use your imagination.

Lastly, it's best to clean up any chairs you may use. Again, your sub will be only too happy to oblige. So, it's always a good idea to make sure that you keep any furniture you use nice and clean. That way, you won't have to regret any nasty smells later on.

## What to Expect With Bathroom Play

Bathroom play is one of those extreme fetishes. Not all folks are inclined to it though most FEMDOMS experiment with it at some point. So, if you are grossed out by it, it's probably best not to engage in it. Also, you might want to refrain from getting too messy if you are sick to your stomach. After all, that could create a very nasty mess that might send everyone over the edge.

On the whole, bathroom play is the kind of kink you can use to humiliate your subs. Some FEMDOMS like to use it as an alternative to cuckoldry. Others like to include it as a part of cuckoldry. As you can see, the theme here is to use the tactics we have been presenting as you see fit. There is nothing wrong with using your imagination. Of course, if you have a sub that's begging for it, then why not give it a try? Some guys love this type of fetish. So, it only makes sense to try it out. Who knows, you might find something truly interesting!

# Part IV: Advanced FEMDOM Tactics

# Chapter 13: Torture Tactics

After mastering the basics, it's time to move on to some really heavy-duty stuff. In the world of FEMDOM, it's quite common to use torture tactics as a means of keeping subs happy. Many of the tactics used in FEMDOM are essentially the same as those used in BDSM. So, if you are familiar with BDSM, then you can appreciate the way FEMDOM uses them. The main difference is that you have a dedicated male sub on the receiving end of torture.

Torture tactics are used mainly as a means of arousal more than humiliation. Also, torture tactics are used as a means of punishing subs. When used as punishment, they need to be harsh enough to create a psychological impact on the sub so that they understand what the consequences of their misbehavior are.

That is why this chapter is focused on looking into the main torture tactics used in FEMDOM and how you can play around with them so that you can suit them to your individual style of play. Please keep in mind that these tactics can be customized to suit your particular preferences. As a result, there is no right or wrong way of going about it. They are just there for you to make them your own.

## Bondage

We had to start here, right?

For newbies, bondage provides an enormous rush. This implies being tied up, literally, handcuffed and shackled. In some cases, mistresses simply tie up their subs and leave them there to contemplate life. Some mistresses slap a mask on their bound sub and let him sit there for a while.

Now, bondage can get as creative as you like it to. There are tables that resemble hospital beds. So, the rails on the sides can be outfitted with handcuffs or shackles. Leather shackles are far more comfortable than metal ones. In fact, metal shackles provide a more realistic experience if you will. Some more creative FEMDOMS like to get antique shackles. When it comes to antique shackles, the rustier, the better.

Then there are boards that can be used to tie up your sub. These boards can be upright so that your sub is standing, while others resemble a wheel. There are some which actually spin. These are pretty entertaining as you can place your sub upside down. They can be part of pretty gruesome torture as hanging upside down for a while can get pretty painful.

Also, subs can be tied to chairs. Earlier, we described the use of the bottomless chair. There are some chairs which are already outfitted for this purpose. However, you can just get an old chair and use ropes. If you prefer chains, then these will do perfectly fine. Some FEMDOMS like to leave their subs tied up in a chair as part of their initial training. It can be fun to leave a tied-up sub to figure out what to do.

If you have a dungeon area, then you can really get creative. For instance, old brick houses have pretty nasty basements. So, shackles can be outfitted to the wall. That will really give the impression that the sub is in a real dungeon. Alternatively, chains that are bolted into the wall can give the sub some room to move though they wouldn't be able to get very far. Additionally, you can shackle both arms and legs. Thus, you can fully restrain your sub.

Some FEMDOMS like to hogtie their subs. To do this, you can use a regular rope to tie your sub's hands behind their back and then tie up their legs with the same rope. This allows the sub to have both hands and feet bound behind their back. They can then be placed on their belly or on their side. If you add a
116

mask and/or ball gag, you have a perfectly helpless sub. There are leather restraints that are already outfitted for this purpose. So, you can simply latch on the cuffs to hands and feet, and your sub is all tied up in a jiffy.

## Cock and Ball Bondage

This is a very specific torture tactic. In this tactic, you are placing restraints on the penis and testicle area. Naturally, this sounds pretty painful. The sub finds himself literally bound by the balls. Depending on the type of device you use, this can get pretty painful.

For example, the use of a cock ring can cause quite a bit of pain. There are various sizes which you can use. So, the smaller kinds don't give the sub much room to maneuver. The larger rings are good for controlling erections. These rings can be quite painful if the sub gets hard because it constricts the penis. As a result, an erection can be quite painful.

One particular type of cock ring is called the "gates of hell." This is a device that has multiple rings that slide onto the length of the penis. These can be quite painful or pleasurable (depending on how you look at it) when the penis is fully erect. It is mainly used as a chastity device though it can be pretty painful if the rings are too small.

Cock rings slide on to the testicles. They create a great deal of pressure in this area. There are various sizes that can constrict the testicles to a greater extent. Thus, the pain can be quite unbearable. The most painful kind are the ones that separate the testicles down the middle. The pressure it creates by separating the balls can be rather uncomfortable after a while. As such, subs can learn valuable lessons through these devices.

Also, there are cages that you can use to fully restrict movement of the penis and create pressure on the testicles. These cages resemble various rings placed together in a triangular shape. This device is designed to constrict both the penis and the testicles. Needless to say, the use of a cage can make it quite uncomfortable for your sub.

## Cock and Ball Torture

Alright, with this type of torture, you are actually getting pretty physical. Here, you are literally poking, pinching, stretching, piercing, and even stepping on the testicles and penis. If you combine this with cock and ball rings, you can practically demolish your sub's genitalia.

For starters, pinching your sub's balls can be a great place to start. This may include using your fingernails (especially if they are long) to pinch the scrotum, or devices such as clamps to actually squash your sub's balls. The use of clothespins can create a similar feeling. Additionally, you can use tweezers to pinch your sub's balls. One creative use of tweezers is to pull hairs out. This can be quite painful after a while.

Other forms of cock and ball torture include stretching. Stretching generally refers to stretching the penis though it can also be done to the testicles. This type of torture can get pretty creative as you can do something simple like using your hands, or a stretching device. Some of these devices resemble a vice. With such a device, you turn a knob or handle, and the device automatically stretches the penis and/or testicles. Another particularly brutal type of torture is to attach a weight to the genitalia. The naturally hangs down, thereby stretching out the testicles or pulling the penis out as far as it will go. Some of the more creative devices use a rope and pulley system. These are common in dungeons and create an interesting visual effect, especially for films.

Then, there is piercing.

Piercing generally refers to the foreskin and scrotum. It is not common to actually pierce the penis and testicles as this could cause severe injury. To do this, any number of devices can be used. The main point is to cause sharp pain in the area that is being pierced. Needles are a popular device used in this type of torture. For instance, regular sewing needles (not surgical) can be used to pierce through the foreskin (not the actual penis) or poke at the scrotum. Needless to say, this can be quite painful. Most mistresses like to put a mask on their subs during this type of torture in order to muffle sounds.

Also, other less conventional devices such as a staple remover can be used to both pinch and pierce through the skin. Some of the most creative torture tactics involve the use of nails (the kind that are used in construction) and staples. Imagine stapling your sub's foreskin to their scrotum!

Of course, it's important that you be careful as piercing may cause bleeding. So, if there is a lot of bleeding, then you may have to deal with the blood loss before proceeding. Also, it's a good practice to disinfect tools before piercing. The last thing you want to cause is an infection. Although, make sure that your sub doesn't know about it. After all, they are there to be tortured.

## Anal Torture

Anal torture differs from anal play. Anal play is a fun activity in which subs get penetrated like little sissies, and that's it. They may be penetrated by a dildo, a strap-on, or even another mal. In this case, we are going to be looking at anal torture. So, we are going to take things to the extreme in this case. Please note that this type of torture can be really painful. That's why the use of masks is quite common. That way, your subs can scream out if they wish. Otherwise, the use of a gag may also work well.

Anal torture is generally caused by inserting some kind of device into the anus of a sub. Needless to say, this can be quite painful in subs who don't have much experience with anal play. Plus, anal play is rather humiliating to most subs. So, everyone wins.

The most common type of anal torture is penetration. However, this type of penetration can be done without lubrication. Needless to say, that is not fun. Without lubrication, the insertion of any object can be quite rough. If you are using a rubber dildo or strap-on, it can be quite tough to gain insertion. In the case of a glass or metal dildo, it might slide it a bit easier.

Also, the use of large devices is a good torture. For instance, large-size butt plugs can be quite painful. The sub must open up pretty wide to take the bulk of the butt plug and then hold it. A butt plug can be used in combination with cock and ball torture. Thus, this creates an excruciating experience.

Additionally, rough and/or violent penetration is a good way of showing dominance. You can ride your sub while wearing a strap-on or perhaps have another male penetrate them, such as in the case of cuckoldry. Rough anal play might not be as bad, but it does create a powerful psychological impact.

Subs may be placed on their hands and knees, that is on all fours, they may be restrained in some manner, or they may be placed lying face on a bed, table or couch. Generally speaking, there is some kind of restraint involved, though if your sub can handle it, they may be allowed to have use of their hands.

One interesting device which could be used is a fuck machine. This is a mechanical device that mimics the thrusting motion of a person during intercourse. When used for anal torture, a fuck machine can unleash a relentless assault on your sub. Naturally, this can get pretty painful after a while. You can combine this device with other types of torture or just use it for your own amusement.

## Getting Creative

Ultimately, torture tactics are about being as creative as you can. Many FEMDOMS evolve their torture tactics to suit their personal tastes. Some like to claw their subs while others may use biting. Some like to pummel their subs by slapping or spanking them. There really is no limit to what you can do so long as your subs don't get injured. This is the main thing to keep in mind here. As long as you don't cause any serious harm or injury to your subs, they'll get over a few bruises.

The only practice we do not recommend is cutting. While some FEMDOMS may engage in this, we don't recommend it. Cutting can be dangerous, as you may cause severe bleeding, although it is quite common in some vampiric practices as it is a form of bloodletting. However, this can be dangerous for both the health of the sub and may cause infection. So, proceed at your own peril.

Beyond that, torture is the most exciting part of the FEMDOM experience for both subs and doms. Don't hold back as subs enjoy pain. They have a masochistic streak that enables them to get aroused from the whole ordeal. And after some good old torture fun, you might be inclined to cap things off with a good round of sexual intercourse. Why not? You've earned it.

# Chapter 14: Anal Play

Up to this point, we have discussed anal play quite extensively. We have discussed it as a means of humiliating your subs, punishing them, and even torturing them. As such, we will now focus on more specific types of anal play which you can use for your own amusement, or perhaps to further inflict torture on your subs. The best part of all is that you can use your creativity to suit your particular tastes.

With that in mind, let's get on with some interesting games you can play with your subs.

## Anal Play Can Be Very Pleasurable

On the surface, anal play seems like it's all about domination and humiliation. And while that is true, it can also be quite pleasurable for a sub.

Allow us to elaborate on this point.

So, being penetrated anally can be quite humiliating and downright emasculating for a male. It makes them feel powerless while apparently stripping them of their masculinity. This is why you hear a lot about prison rape. When inmates are raped by other males, most people associate this with some kind of deviant sexual perversion. The fact is that there really isn't anything sexual about prison rape. It's mainly a question of asserting power among the prison hierarchy.

This is an important point to keep in mind. While engaging in anal play is about having fun and enjoying yourself, the main purpose of doing this is to assert your dominance as the FEMDOM. If we take it even further, it can be about completely stripping your sub of his masculinity. This is especially important when you have powerful men who like to be helpless sissies when in your clutches.

Surprisingly, anal play can be quite pleasurable for a sub. You see, the prostate gland can be stimulated from behind, that is, through the rectum. When this occurs, the stimulation to the prostate can lead to uncontrollable orgasm and ejaculation. In some sexual practices, females are taught to insert their fingers into the male's anus and stimulate the prostate. This is done as an alternative means of sexual pleasure.

In this case, you are actually giving your sub a welcome treat, and you can stimulate their prostate gland as part of the entire anal play dynamic. So yes, they do have to put up with the pain of the insertion. But ultimately, they derive a benefit from it. Because of this, you can use anal play as a risk-reward type deal. They must go through the pain of being penetrated, but the end result will be quite pleasurable.

To ensure that you hit the prostate, a longer dildo or strap-on would be needed. Short and stubby dildos or butt plugs won't do the job. You would need something longer, regardless of its thickness, to ensure that you hit the mark. You can tell if you're in the right spot as your sub will come to enjoy the effect.

## Anal Training

When you're dealing with a new sub, they will most likely be unfamiliar or unaccustomed to anal play. There is nothing wrong with that. If anything, it just means that they don't have much experience with this type of play. In fact, you'll find that some guys ask their wives and girlfriends to engage in anal play with them. Most women are freaked out by a request of this nature. In fact, they may even suspect their man to be gay when, in reality, they are only seeking a different type of rush. This is why a great deal of subs seek out mistresses who can oblige them.

With that in mind, anal play can be quite fun for your sub(s), but you can't really expect them to handle everything you throw at them, at least not right away. So, here's are some helpful tips for anal training your new subs.

First, make regular use of butt plugs. At first, the shorter, thinner kind can work well. You can require your sub to wear a butt plug through their regular day. In doing so, you may even lead to bathroom control. For instance, the sub cannot go to the bathroom for a certain amount of time. This is meant to ensure that they keep the butt plug in place as part of their training.

Then, you may also require your subs to wear anal beads. These are inserted all the way up the rectum.

At the tail end of the beads, there is a string that is pulled on to remove them. This helps to stretch out the anal cavity, thereby facilitating penetration. Plus, they can be rather uncomfortable, especially if you are sitting at your desk all day.

Anal beads and butt plugs come in all sizes. So, you can gradually move up from the smaller sizes up to the bigger ones. This type of practice can make it seems like your sub is "graduating" from one size to another. The great thing about this type of exercise is that you don't need to be there with them to ensure that they are training their butt hole.

While your sub is in your presence, you can devote specific time to training his butt. If the sub is clearly not ready for full penetration, you can progressively stretch out their butt hole by using a combination of dildos. Some mistresses like to start out their new subs with thinner dildos and progressively use thicker ones. As your sub's butthole gets stretched out, you can certainly make good use of bigger and bigger dildos. In fact, you may even use a larger dildo to pleasure yourself as a means of visual teasing, and then use that dildo on your sub. In a manner of speaking, it's like, "do you like what you see? Okay, now it's your turn!"

Lastly, be careful if you use other types of objects in your sub's butt. For instance, vegetables are commonly used though they may break during intense play. Also, avoid wooden objects as they may splinter, thereby causing injury. Anything that's sharp or pointed may cause internal bleeding. Also, anything that has a rough texture to it might also cause considerable injury. So, it's best to stay on the safe side.

## Being Penetrated By Another Male

This practice can really drive your subs over the edge. Throughout this book, we have discussed this possibility as a means of extreme humiliation, such as in the case of cuckoldry. On the whole, having your subs penetrated by another male can be a pretty extreme form of punishment.

So, let's take a look at two scenarios here.

The first is to have another male (hetero, bi, or homosexual) join the fun. This male would be in charge of penetrating the sub(s). Now, it is important to note the presence of multiple subs as having the others watch what happens to one can create a pretty tough mental picture.

In this situation, you can even play games. For instance, you can draw straws or turn a roulette wheel. The sub whose number comes up would get the business. This can be quite exciting for spectators and pretty gruesome for the subs taking part. If you only have one sub present, you can spin the wheel to see if they get a dildo, strap-on, or the other male. This type of humiliation game can get even more extreme when engaging in cuckoldry. If anything, having a game such as a spinning a wheel can produce a humorous tone to what would otherwise be a pretty intense moment.

The second scenario would be to have the third male pick his sub. This works very well when the third mal doesn't know who the subs are, and while the subs are wearing masks. As such, the third male can take his pick of whoever he wants.

This particular scenario can be amplified to have a number of subs with multiple FEMDOMS and males present. In a manner of speaking, it's like having a FEMDOM party. There are some parties in which masters and mistresses come together to have their pick of subs. In fact, you might even enjoy swapping out subs for an evening. These types of parties are rather common and generally happen on an invitation basis only. So, if you get on well with other FEMDOMS or take party in a FEMDOM community, you may very well get an invite to one of these parties. However, if you are in a committed relationship with your sub, you might want to think twice about taking part in such a party.

At these parties, you'll find that masters enjoy penetrating multiple subs. This tactic is quite useful as part of a humiliation game, or just as a means for the master to please himself. Mistresses may also take the time to penetrate multiple subs. This could be part of a party game, or simply as part of a sub initiation. In such cases, some FEMDOMS require their subs to go through some sort of initiation ritual. In some circumstances, this may include taking part in a party and being "served" to others doms in their community.

## What If Your Sub Is Not Into Anal Play?

By definition, being a sub means you are willing to oblige to anything your mistress wants. As such, subs can't really say no to much. This implies that they must be compliant, or else they would lose their sub status.

This opens up an interesting path.

There are some guys who only dabble superficially in the world of FEMDOM. So, they only seek a dominatrix to walk them around like a puppy and whip them up a couple of times a month. This means that they are not fully committed to being subs. In such cases, you may find that these are men who are only looking to experiment with the FEMDOM world.

When a man is only looking to experiment, they are most likely looking to see if it's right for them. If that's the case, then you can't really blame them for not wanting to engage in certain practices. This is what differentiates the true subs from the guys who are only experimenting.

So, if you have a sub who is willing to go along, but reluctant to actually open up, you may want to go easy on him. So, the use of butt plugs and anal beads can be a good introduction to the world of anal play. You might want to lay off the heavier stuff until they are truly ready to go that route. Please bear in mind that one of the roles a dom plays in any power relationship is to guide their sub down the path of both pleasure and pain. Consequently, you can instruct your sub on how they can learn to love the pain they feel.

In the event that you are in a committed relationship, then you can determine whether certain anal play tactics are off-limits. For instance, you may be perfectly comfortable with penetrating your sub yourself, but completely against having someone else do it. In that case, then you can set the boundaries as the FEMDOM.

Ultimately, your decision to engage in anal play largely depends on your personality and how far you want to take things. Some FEMDOMS are perfectly happy with having a slave who just wants to serve his mistress and take a dildo up the butt every so often. Then, there are situations in which you can really turn the heat up.

It's up to you!

There is no one here to tell you what you should do. It's all a question of doing what is most comfortable and natural to you.

# Chapter 15: BDSM Play

Throughout this book, we have mentioned BDSM as part of the FEMDOM dynamic. While it is generally incorporated into FEMDOM, it's not a requirement to engage in BDSM as a part of FEMDOM. In fact, you can have a rather "light" version of FEMDOM in which you don't engage in any type of BDSM play. These types of "light" FEMDOM relationships may include humiliation tactics like cuckoldry and anal play but without the dungeon or bondage setup.

In general terms, BDSM stands for "bondage, discipline, submission, masochism." As you can see, it's a pretty large term that encompasses a number of practices. So, associating BDSM to just bondage is only a part of the story. When you "discipline" a sub, you are engaging in BDSM play. If your sub enjoys pain, then that's BDSM play as well.

On the whole, BDSM is characterized by bondage and torture. But then again, that's only one approach to the traditional way of approaching the FEMDOM dynamic. As such, the classic depiction of the latex-covered dominatrix is only one way of making BDSM work in practice.

In this chapter, we are going to look at the four components of BDSM and the various ways in which you can incorporate them into your usual FEMDOM practices.

## Bondage and Restraint

Typically, bondage is seen as tying up subs in a dungeon while menacing doms torture them senseless. While that is only one way of going about it, there are many different ways of approaching bondage. So, let's take a look at them going from relatively mild bondage scenarios to rather extreme ones.

To get started, simple restraint tactics like handcuffing a sub to a bed rail can provide enough excitement. You may choose to restrain the sub's hands only or restrain both hands and legs. There are kits that can be retrofitted to any type of bed. Otherwise, you may purchase a bed frame that would specifically lend itself to this type of setup. Alternatively, a hospital bed with the rails on both sides serves this purpose very well. Some rather simple bondage scenes depict a sub handcuffed, or shackled, to the bed, wearing a mask, while the mistress has her way with the sub. This may seem rather mild compared to some of the stuff we have talked about throughout this book, but it's a fun scenario that regular couples love to explore.

Earlier, we mentioned the use of surgical tables. These tables can be used very well in a space where you can leave it there. For example, if you have a workshop in your garage, you can set up a table like this for the purpose of BDSM. Folks who outfit their basement for BDSM play like to leave a table in a corner where they can have their fun.

When using a table, it's important to make sure that it's pretty sturdy as it would have to support quite a bit of weight in addition to any struggling or squirming. So, using your kitchen table may not be the best option in this case.

Some bondage practitioners like to use old doctor's examination tables, especially the ones with stirrups. That way, you can have clear access to your sub's nether regions. They make for some very interesting bondage scenes, especially if you want to explore a doctor-patient bondage scene.

Then, there are chairs.

The basic, bottomless chair we have discussed earlier can serve quite well for bondage play. Older metal chairs, the heavier ones, work really well for this type of play. Generally speaking, they serve very well when it comes to keeping your sub from moving around more than they should.

It's when you look at specially designed chairs that things get really crazy.

For starters, there are chairs that look like a demented dentist's chair. Some have stirrups while others have armrest with cuffs on them and chains for leg shackles. These chairs are reclinable and allow the FEMDOM access to all parts of the sub.

There are other chairs which have a "T" shape. The chair itself is a normal chair with leg restraints. However, the "T" shape is used to restrain the arm.

So, you have the sub in a sitting position with arms stretched out. This allows for an excruciating position. Also, you have access to your sub's entire body.

In addition, you'll find a chair that resembles a throne. However, it's essentially a medieval torture device as it has armrests with restraints (some have restraints in the back so that the sub's arms are tied behind the backrest) and leg shackles. But here is where they get really insane. Some have the option of adding a dildo or other type of device on which the sub must sit on. Others have an open hole that gives access to the sub's genital area. These chairs provide very little comfort and are intended to increase pain after prolonged sitting.

Lastly, there are some chairs that are built so that the sub's front is tied to the backrest of the chair. Essentially, it appears as though the sub is sitting with the chair turned around backward. This position exposes the sub's backside, thus giving the FEMDOM free access. This position is very good for anal play. You could also engage in cock and ball torture if you fancy.

When using chairs, make sure that the chair won't slip or tip over. If it does, it could cause a great deal of damage to your sub. Needless to say, this is something that is best avoided. So, do keep this in mind when setting up your chair. In some cases, they are bolted to the floor, while in others, they are pegged up against a wall. That way, no amount of struggling would tip the chair over.

# Discipline, Submission, and Masochism

By now, you are well-versed in the ways of discipline and submission. You know exactly how to treat your sub(s), and most importantly, how to discipline them should the need arise. It's important to note that when you threaten a sub, it's important to follow through. For instance, if you say to a sub, "don't do that or else," then you had better mean it.

Often, discipline is just a question of being firm in your decisions. When you threaten a sub and follow through, the sub will have no choice but to take your word for it every time. This can be a bit tough with new subs, as they may not be entirely clear on your expectations. This is why you must be tough on them at all times. Otherwise, your subs won't learn to respect your rules.

Additionally, subs are masochists. Otherwise, they wouldn't be willing to engage in the practice they are involved in. They enjoy the pain they feel. They derive pleasure from being pounded by a dominant figure. While it's true that some male subs seek a male dom, they also seek out female doms as this helps to fill a void they are missing. In fact, don't be surprised to find high-ranking folks, businesspeople, and rich individuals seeking out this kind of thrill. In many ways, it makes them feel alive. Also, it may just be that they are bored with their usual sex life and are seeking something new.

For what it's worth, you have something that these individuals seek. You can provide them with the ultimate experience. As such, don't go easy on them. Take your subs as far as they will go. You will find that subs can generally tolerate a great deal of pain and punishment. Once they recover, they'll keep coming back for more. It might sound counterintuitive, but the average individual seeks the rush that comes with being manhandled by a dominant female.

As we have mentioned throughout this book, use your imagination. There is no shortage of ideas that you can come up with. If anything, subs will remain faithful to you, the more creative you get. So, go off the deep end if you wish!

# Conclusion

Thank you very much for making all the way to the end of this book. We hope that you have been inspired by the ideas we have presented herein. The world of FEMDOM is an exciting domain which is so vast. There is no shortage of wonderful ideas which you can put into practice. In fact, don't be surprised if your sub(s) come up with some kinky ideas of their own.

At this point, you are ready to run your own show. If you are new or relatively inexperienced in this type of play, don't worry. The most important thing at this point is to develop your own personality. As you do this, you will find what tactics turn you on, and also, what tactics turn your subs on.

In the event that you are exploring FEMDOM as part of a committed relationship, it's always good to talk things over before truly committing to it. Often, being on the same page makes this experience the best that it can be. However, if you neglect to agree on the fundamentals, you might not get the results you seek.

On the whole, the FEMDOM dynamic is empowering and can help you truly explore your dominant side. As a female dom, you are the one in charge of running the show. As such, you have the power to turn any man into a quivering coward. Don't feel sorry for them. Many guys crave that experience. After all, they are truly subs. The thing is that they have been unable to let themselves express their weaker side. So, in the privacy of a FEMDOM dungeon, they can show just how weak they truly are.

We hope you have enjoyed this book. If you felt it was useful and informative, do tell others who may be interested in it. We want nothing more than the FEMDOM community to grow. There are plenty of powerful females out there and countless weak men who seek the control of a powerful female. If that sounds like you, then go for it! You have everything to gain from exploring your dominant side.

# Description

Have you ever experienced the rush that comes with dominating your sexual partner?

Have you ever experienced the power trip you get with submitting your sexual partner to your will?

Have you ever experienced the adrenaline you get with seeing your sexual partner helpless while begging you for mercy?

Have you ever experienced the satisfaction that comes with reducing your sexual partner to a quivering coward?

If you can relate to these questions, then it's time you explored your darker side. In this book, we are going to explore the world of FEMDOM and how you can take your naturally dominant side and transform yourself into a powerful mistress. With the information presented in this book, you will get an introduction into the world of FEMDOM and how you can turn your man into dust.

For a lot of gals out there, this is the ultimate fantasy. There is nothing more stimulating and gratifying than to see your partner tied up, beating, and subdued. In fact, the rush of power that comes from having your partner completely helpless is incredibly difficult to beat.

In this volume you will learn about:

1. The world and FEMDOM and how you can become a powerful mistress without much difficulty
2. How to train your male subs so that they are reduced into a shaking maggot
3. The ways in which you can set up your personal domain to reflect your dominant personality
4. The types of outfits you can wear to suit your taste and personal style
5. The ways in which you can subject your male subs to excruciating torture and humiliation
6. The use of props and devices which you can put to good use during your FEMDOM scenes and encounters
7. The use of chairs and tables in your domination scenes
8. How you can use bathroom play to really take things up a notch while reducing your sub to nothing
9. How to use torture effectively especially as a means of punishment
10. Cuckoldry and other humiliation tactics

... and so much more!

So, if you have been thinking about unleashing your dark side, then there is no time like the present. If you are into BDSM, you will find that this book covers this topic extensively. In fact, we'll give you so many ideas; you won't even know where to begin.

We know that you are eager to get started with your FEMDOM fantasies. We are also sure that there are plenty of men out there who are eager to be your submissive slaves. So, why not oblige? Make them your slaves by pummeling them into submission.

Do you know what the best part is?

They'll keep coming back for more. Your subs will be so thrilled by the tactics you have for them, that they won't be able to stay away. In fact, don't be surprised if you get requests from multiple subs.

What are you waiting for?

Let's get started in the world of FEMDOM today! A word of caution though: once you cross the threshold, you won't be able to go back...